Don't . . . Touch . . . Me!

"You never used to say that," Brand said.

"Circumstances are quite different now," Melody flung at him.

This time his jaw hardened at her words.

"You're absolutely right," he said. "They're very different. You've got the power either to send your brother to prison or to keep him free."

A chill climbed Melody's spine and her hands felt suddenly icy. "Wh-what do I have to do?"

"You have to marry me again," he said in a voice of steel. "You may as well resign yourself to the fact. I'm ready to be a generous and agreeable husband to you, but if you continue to cross me, you'll find me a dangerous enemy.

SONDRA STANFORD

fell in love with the written word as soon as she could read one, at the age of six. However, besides her writing ability, she is also a gifted painter and it was a "struggle to decide which talent would dominate." Fortunately for all her Silhouette readers the written word triumphed!

Dear Reader:

Silhouette Romances is an exciting new publishing venture. We will be presenting the very finest writers of contemporary romantic fiction as well as outstanding new talent in this field. It is our hope that our stories, our heroes and our heroines will give you, the reader, all you want from romantic fiction.

Also, *you* play an important part in our future plans for Silhouette Romances. We welcome any suggestions or comments on our books and I invite you to write to us at the address below.

So, enjoy this book and all the wonderful romances from Silhouette. They're for *you*!

P. J. Fennell
President and Publisher
Silhouette Books
P.O. Box 769
New York, N.Y. 10019

SONDRA STANFORD

Golden Tide

Published by Silhouette Books New York

For my parents and for Cash, who first
encouraged me on this journey

SILHOUETTE BOOKS, a Simon & Schuster Division of
GULF & WESTERN CORPORATION
1230 Avenue of the Americas, New York, N.Y. 10020

Distributed by Pocket Books

ISBN: 0-671-57006-4

First Silhouette printing May, 1980

10 9 8 7 6 5 4 3 2 1

Printed in the U.S.A.

Chapter One

"How on earth do they expect anyone to eat a meal when they're jammed up at a small table with a bunch of strangers? Reminds me of a herd of cattle at round-up time," Dale Upton grumbled into his sister's ear.

Melody Travers giggled. At least Dale was fortunate enough to be seated at the end of the table. She was wedged between him and a rather stout lady on her left. "It's not arranged for comfort," she conceded in a whisper so that her voice would not carry to her neighbor. "I'm practically sitting in this poor lady's lap."

Dale surveyed the table with an air of disgust. "Just wait until the rest of the people arrive," he growled in a low voice. "When they fill those chairs opposite us, we'll be eyeball to eyeball instead of just elbow to elbow. All I can say is that the food had better be good . . . as well as the show!"

"Regretting your offer to bring me already, huh?" Melody jibed with a teasing smile.

Her brother gave her a reluctant grin. "Almost," he admitted. "I *would* rather be at the crap tables."

"They'll still be there when the show is over," Melody said without sympathy, "so stop complaining. You know the only reason I came out here with you was because you promised we'd take in some good shows."

"And I'm keeping my promise," Dale pointed out as he reached into his pocket for a cigarette, "so you'd better appreciate me! There aren't many brothers who would suffer this kind of squeeze for a mere sister, you know."

Melody laughed, and while Dale lit his cigarette she glanced around the room with interest. It was of enormous proportions, with as many tables and chairs crammed into it as was possible, and already practically every table was filled. Despite his grumbling, she and Dale sat at

5

a table near the stage, where they would be afforded an excellent view of the performance once it began. Luck had had nothing to do with that, however. Melody had seen a sizable sum of money being exchanged between Dale and the maitre d'.

Her attention was drawn back to her brother by the impatient drumming of his fingers against the table. He was anxious for the meal to arrive, the show to start. He was eager to return to the casino and that, Melody knew, was exactly what he would do once he considered that he had done his duty to his sister by escorting her to this dinner show.

Beneath the shield of long lashes she stole a glance at his profile. At twenty-nine, Dale was a rather handsome man with ear-length dark brown hair and light brown eyes. His face was youthfully rounded, which had always been his despair, and he wore a thick moustache, which Melody hated, in an effort to appear more mature.

The two of them did not look much alike. Her own hair, worn shoulder length and curled, was a russet brown and her wide-set eyes were green with tiny flecks of brown and gold. Melody considered Dale the better looking, for he took their mother's looks while she favored their father, inheriting his squarish chin that gave her a too-stubborn appearance to ever lend real beauty. She had been told a number of times by men that she was beautiful, but she had always taken their words with a grain of salt, since her own mirror told her a different story. She was totally unconscious of the devastating effect of wide green eyes thickly fringed with sooty lashes, generous, soft lips, and a chin that bespoke character and that appealed to men as valiant and spirited rather than stubborn.

Until yesterday she had not seen Dale in over a year and a half, and she decided now that he had not changed at all since the last time they had been together. He was still as lighthearted and ready to have a good time as he had been years ago when they had been teenagers. The only thing

6

she had ever known Dale to be intense about had been his job and that, despite himself, had been a great success.

But an instant later, she mentally revised her assessment as he began recounting a blackjack game he had played that afternoon. She listened with the same chilling dismay that had affected her earlier when she had stood watching him gamble. Dale had behaved as though it were a life-or-death matter, going far beyond just gambling a few dollars merely to have fun, and it had frightened her. It was a side of him she was seeing for the first time and she didn't like it at all. Intensity about business was one thing; that same intensity over a game of chance was rather terrifying. She wondered whether or not it had been a mistake to come to Las Vegas after all.

It had sounded like fun when Dale had telephoned her in Dallas last week and first proposed the trip. He had a couple of weeks of vacation coming, he had told her, and planned to spend a few days of it in Vegas, so why didn't she come along with him? Melody had accepted at once. She was overdue for a vacation herself, and though Rob had been completely against the idea, she had refused to let his disapproval deter her. Besides, she had asked him, what harm could possibly come from spending a few days relaxing with her own brother? It had taken some persuading, but at last he had agreed that the office could do without her for at least a week.

Yesterday had been fun, but at the same time rather exhausting. Melody had met Dale's incoming plane at the Dallas airport and later in the day they had boarded another flight together bound for Las Vegas.

The trip had passed quickly because they were so busy catching up on one another's news. Dale told her how his work was going and had laughingly described a few girls he was currently dating, though he said he still had no plans for marriage. That led them to a discussion of their widowed father's recent remarriage to a lady neither of them had yet met, for since his retirement from a naval

7

career a few years earlier, he had moved permanently to Spain. Dale quizzed her about Rob and her job and they thoroughly enjoyed one another's company. There was only one subject they kept strictly away from, as they had for the past five years, and though there were many questions in Melody's mind, she would never ask them. There were some things it was better not to know.

"Too bad your lawyer couldn't get away and come with us," Dale said now, bringing her back to the present. "I feel I should meet him and look him over, what with Dad across the world and out of pocket."

Melody bristled slightly. "Look him over? You sound as though you have the right to approve or disapprove, but you don't. I'd like you to meet Rob, Dale, but I'll marry him whether you like him or not. I'm no giddy eighteen-year-old with stardust blinding her eyes this time!"

"You're twenty-five and all grown up." Dale nodded and crushed his cigarette in the ashtray. "How cynical you sound, Mel. But no matter what you say, you're still my baby sister. I just don't want to see you make another mistake with your life."

"Don't worry." She sighed and began twisting her water glass between the palms of her hands with an unconscious nervous gesture. "I'm not rushing into anything. I've been Rob Wallis's secretary now for almost three years, so I'd say we know each other well enough. Rob is completely different in every way from . . ."

"Brand!" Dale exclaimed in a shocked voice.

Melody's head jerked up and her hands dropped the water glass with a thud, causing some of the water to slosh out onto the tablecloth. She stared, blinked her eyes disbelievingly, and stared again as a tight vise squeezed her chest and almost totally cut off her breathing.

Dale had shoved back his chair and stood up and was reaching across the table to shake hands with the man they had just been discussing. And then both men sat down, Dale beside Melody, her former husband just opposite her.

8

"Good evening, Melody," Brand Travers said in a polite voice, while his eyes lowered from her face to the V plunge in the neckline of the green dress she was wearing.

Melody's face reddened with anger at his deliberately insulting action, and beneath the covers of the tablecloth she knotted her fists in her lap. "Hello, Brand," she said in a flat, dull voice. "What a surprise to meet you here."

"Yes," Dale agreed, but with far more enthusiasm in his voice. "It is a surprise, Brand. This can't be a coincidence. Did you come out here to find me?"

Brand's insolent gaze finally shifted from Melody to Dale, and after an imperceptible moment, he nodded. "Yes," he said. "I came to find you."

"What's wrong?" Dale demanded anxiously. "Surely that Bateman account in New Orleans didn't fall through? I had it sewed up, Brand!"

"As far as I know the Bateman account is still sewed up," Brand answered carelessly as he now swung his gaze to the side, surveying the room himself as Melody had earlier.

"Then what is it?" Dale asked tensely.

Melody looked at him in surprise. Even during her initial state of shock over seeing Brand again, she had noticed that her brother had been pleased to see him, but now he seemed somewhat upset.

Brand finally looked at him again, and there was a thoughtful expression in his coal-black eyes. But instead of answering Dale's question, after a moment he shook his head. "It's a rather personal matter between us," he said now, "and I think you'd rather we discussed it in the privacy of my hotel room after the show is over."

"P-personal?" Dale echoed, and again Melody glanced at him curiously. Was Dale nervous of his own employer? It certainly seemed that way.

Quickly, she tried to smooth over the awkward moment. "It's all right, Dale," she said. "What Brand means, I'm sure, is that whatever he came to speak to you about is none of my business."

"Not at all," Brand responded, totally confounding her. "I'd like you to sit in on our meeting, if you don't mind. It concerns you as well. But"—now he glanced meaningfully down the length of the table at the other people who were all total strangers—"I just feel we'd do better to have our discussion in a quieter place."

At that moment, the waiter appeared to take their orders for dinner, and the discussion had to be dropped. And for the remainder of the time, during dinner and until the show actually started, Brand kept up a stream of meaningless, polite small talk, sometimes with her and sometimes with Dale.

Melody was hard put to respond with the same degree of cool civility. Apparently Brand felt not the least awkward at meeting his ex-wife after a period of five years, but, then, Melody had never developed his degree of smooth sophistication. Besides, she was still suffering from shock at suddenly being confronted by him like this, while he must have known she was here with Dale from the start, since he had said his business here concerned her as well.

She frowned as the meal finally drew to an end and the waiter brought coffee. What kind of business could she and Brand possibly have together after this many years? It didn't make the least sense. When she had left him, Dale had continued on in his employ, but otherwise they had no personal connection with each other at all. The slate between them had been wiped carefully blank.

Melody lifted her eyelashes and studied Brand covertly from across the narrow table. He was having an after-dinner cigarette with his coffee and his hand held the cigarette just over the ashtray only inches from her. She could easily have reached out her hand and touched his if she had had a mind to do so. Those hands that had touched her so intimately . . .

With a jerk, she halted the headlong flight of her thoughts into forbidden regions and now she studied his face. He was leaning toward Dale, listening to something

10

he was saying, so for the moment, at least, she could look at him unobserved. Brand appeared little different from what she had remembered. His tall-six-foot-three-inch frame was still rock hard and lean. There was a quality of firmly controlled, unleashed energy about him, and he still possessed that aura of sexual magnetism that had so completely affected her senses when they had been married. Her gaze flickered across his chest and shoulders. The superb cut of his dark suit jacket spread smoothly over his wide chest and broad shoulders, doing nothing to conceal the strength she knew was there. His hair was still as thick as ever, black as Texas oil, except that tonight there was a slight frosting at the temples that had definitely not been there previously. His face, angular and strong, was darkly tanned, but there seemed to be a few lines slashing across his forehead and down his cheekbones that had not been present five years ago. The eyes and mouth had changed the most, she decided. In the past, those dark eyes had usually been alight with loving tenderness or teasing, devilish fun. Now the light had been extinguished; the eyes dark, mysterious pools that gave away nothing of what he was thinking or feeling. And his lips, which she had always considered soft and gentle, were actually hard, chiseled lines.

What had started out as an evening of pleasure became, to Melody, an evening of sheer torture. By the time the famous singer she had so looked forward to seeing actually appeared on the stage, she was in such an overwrought state that she scarcely even heard him. She was far too aware of the tense atmosphere at the table.

And it had become tense, there was no doubt of that. Besides her own shock over being confronted by Brand so unexpectedly, the two men were strained in their attitudes toward each other. There was an intangible, invisible dam between them that had quickly staunched the flow of idle chitchat. Brand had started out polite and casual, and it was Dale who had changed the atmosphere. He had grown increasingly fidgety throughout dinner, only picking at his meal and scarcely even bothering to carry on the light pretense that this was any longer a purely social evening. He smoked too much and there were tighly pinched lines about his mouth that had not been evident before Brand's arrival. And Brand himself seemed to grow quieter and more tense himself.

By the time the show ended at last, Melody wasn't sure she was relieved or not. Her entire body was rigid with taut nerves as she stood up and the three of them slowly weaved their way through the crowd of other patrons toward the exit.

"I have a rental car outside," Brand said from behind her as they reached the casino. "We'll drive back to my hotel, where we can talk in my room."

Melody wanted to object. She was tired and she wanted to go back to their own hotel and go to bed. She stole a quick glance at her brother and it was enough to silence her. His face had gone a pasty white and he looked ill. He pulled out a handkerchief and mopped at his brow.

Without looking at Brand, Melody turned and began to make her way through the casino toward the main door of the hotel, oblivious to the loud din created by the clattering of slot machines and mumbling voices at the blackjack and crap tables.

Once they were outside, the night air was sharp and chilling against her bare arms, and Melody shivered.

"You should have brought a wrap," Brand said in a low voice. She was startled. She had not realized he was so close behind her. Now he reached out and took her arm. "The car is this way," he said smoothly. "Watch the curb here."

Melody jerked free from his grasp. An electrical shock had jolted through her as his hand rested against her skin. "Don't . . . touch . . . me!" She gritted through clenched teeth.

There was not the slightest change in his expression. They had reached the car and as he unlocked the door,

12

Melody glanced back and saw that Dale was trailing a few yards behind them. "You never used to say that," Brand said in a mild voice.

Melody glared at him. "Circumstances are quite different now," she flung at him.

This time his jaw hardened at her words. His body went rigid and then he nodded curtly. "You're absolutely right," he said. "They're very different." And there was such a grim note in his voice that all at once she was frightened.

"Wh-what do you mean?" she whispered.

Brand's eyes met and held hers for only a second and there was a hard, unyielding expression in his. "Get in the car," he said abruptly. He opened the passenger door of the front seat and she had no choice but to slide inside, and as he closed it again, she had the strangest sensation that she was being locked behind prison bars.

Dale sat in the backseat and the three of them were silent as Brand drove the car away from the hotel and entered the busy stream of traffic on the Strip.

Melody stared out the window. The glittering nightime lights of Vegas seemed to mock at her, blinking and winking and teasing, beckoning her to come and enjoy and have a good time, while inside the car the tension was heavy and dark. Something was dreadfully wrong and only she did not know what it was.

By the time they entered Brand's suite a half hour later, Melody was conscious of a throbbing headache, brought on by a fear of some unknown, but nevertheless real, menace.

In the sitting room, Brand waved a careless hand toward the sofa and chairs, indicating they should both sit down, while he swiftly crossed the room, scooped up the telephone, and ordered coffee.

Dale took a chair and Melody dropped down onto the plushly cushioned sofa. Nervously, she began twisting her engagement ring around her finger, and when she looked up, she caught Brand's eyes on her and she froze. There was a hard, cruel twist to his lips as he watched her and in that moment she knew that he hated her, that somehow he intended to hurt her.

Brand cradled the telephone, but instead of coming to join them, he lit a cigarette and walked over to the windows, where he stood gazing out, his shoulders hunched as though he were suddenly very tired.

Dale half-turned in his chair so that he could see Brand. Through stiff, bluish-white lips, he said, "Let's not drag this thing out, Brand. Let's get it over with."

Brand turned slowly and looked at Dale, and Melody was amazed to read sadness on his face. "You know why I wanted to see you, then?" he asked heavily.

Dale nodded. "Yes," he said, his voice taut. "But there's no need to involve Melody in this, is there? Send her out."

Brand shook his head. "No. I want her here. This concerns her, too."

"No!" Dale exploded, jerking to his feet. "Damn it, it does not!"

Brand merely looked at him. "You know," he said softly, "she's got to find out."

Dale flung himself back into his chair and, leaning over, propped his elbows on his knees and dropped his head into his hands in a gesture of absolute despair.

"Will somebody tell me what's going on, for God's sake?" Melody asked in a trembling voice. "I can't stand this much longer!"

A discreet knock came at the door and Brand crossed the room and opened it. A waiter came in with a tray of coffee, and a moment later Brand said, "Pour it for us, please, will you, Melody?"

"What I need," Melody said shakily, "is a good stiff drink, not coffee!" But her little joke, since they all knew she rarely drank, went sadly awry, for neither of the two men so much as smiled.

She poured the coffee. Brand came and sank down at the other end of the sofa, leaving the space empty between them. Melody handed him a cup of the coffee and gave Dale his, and then sat silently, stirring her own.

"Well," Brand said at last, "do you want to start, Dale, or shall I?"

Dale shook his head. "I'm sorry, Brand. It . . . it's all I can say. I'm . . . sorry." He stared at the carpeted floor.

Melody turned slightly so that she was facing Brand. "Tell me," she commanded in a tight voice. "Tell me right now, Brand, before I go crazy."

Brand leaned forward and placed his filled coffee cup on the table. Then he met her eyes levelly and once again she was struck by his obvious unhappiness. Even so, she was in no way prepared for what was to come.

"Dale has been stealing company funds," he told her bluntly.

The color in Melody's face drained away, leaving ghostly skin against the vivid emerald of her dress. The cup and saucer she held clattered as her hand trembled so badly that Brand had to remove it from her resistless fingers. Her eyes darkened with pain and she stared at him as though she had never seen him before in her life.

"I don't believe you!" She gasped in a tortured voice. "No! I don't believe you! You're making this up!" With a volition of their own, her hands went out and began pounding against his chest.

Two strong, sun-browned hands captured hers and brought an end to their attack. "I'm sorry, Melody." Brand's deep voice penetrated through the thick haze of her rage. "There was just no easier way to tell you, and God knows I wish I *were* making it up."

The gentleness of his voice stilled her and she turned to look across at Dale. He was watching them, and as Melody's eyes met his a spasm of shame crossed his handsome, boyish features and once again he lowered his head and stared at the floor.

"Tell me he's lying, Dale!" Melody cried. "Tell me!"

Instead, there was a long silence during which none of them seemed to breathe. Melody's eyes were intent upon her brother, and her heart was willing him to speak up and defend himself. But he did not, and at last she knew it was the truth.

Limply, she pulled her hands away from Brand's and bent her head as she fought back tears. This was worse, much worse, than she could possibly have imagined.

"Why?" she asked in a dull voice, without lifting her head. "Why, Dale? Brand paid you an excellent salary."

"I had gambling debts," he answered flatly.

Melody's head jerked up and her eyes widened. "Gambling debts!"

Dale nodded and lit a cigarette with an unsteady hand. Then, staring at the wall opposite him, he said, "It just stacked up on me through the years and somehow my salary never seemed to be enough to cover it all." He shrugged his shoulders expressively. "As Brand's chief assistant, it was fairly easy to lay my hands on extra money from business trips and expenses connected with various accounts I handled."

"And did you never think you might get caught?" Melody asked bitterly.

Dale shrugged again. "At first the amounts I took were small, so it would have been hard to prove. But after a while I started juggling expense reports to cover larger sums and I . . . I just convinced myself I deserved it. Brand is worth millions, so I decided, why should he chaff at a measly few hundred dollars?"

"Thousands, Dale," Brand quietly corrected.

"Thousands," Dale agreed, nodding. "It never seemed like so much at the time . . . just a little here and a little there." He sucked in a deep breath and then turned to look at Brand. "I'm truly sorry," he said earnestly. "You've been damned good to me through the years. I'm sorry I let you down, but actually, I think I'm relieved it's out in the open now. So"—he sucked in a deep breath—

"what do we do next? Call in the cops here or wait until we get back to Texas?"

"That," said Brand, "depends on Melody."

"Mel?" Dale exclaimed.

"On . . . on me?" Melody stammered, whirling to stare at Brand.

His face was now as colorless as hers and Dale's, but there was a granite hardness to it that proved he was in command. "On you," he reiterated. "You've got the power to either send your brother to prison or to keep him free."

A chill climbed Melody's spine and her hands felt suddenly icy. She licked her dry lips and asked with foreboding, "Wh-what do I have to do?"

"You have to marry me again," he said in a voice of steel.

Melody flinched and pressed back against the arm of the sofa, as far from him as she could get. "You . . . you're joking, of course!" she gasped.

Brand shook his head. "I assure you, I was never more serious in my life. Either you marry me or Dale goes to prison."

Melody glanced at Dale and saw that he was as bewildered as she. "But . . . why?" She asked shakily, forcing herself to face Brand again.

"Because I need someone to help out with Tammy. After you ran away from us, I felt I had no choice but to send her to boarding school—only it hasn't worked out well. She's been forced out of seven different schools. If you come back, she can stay home and go to school like a normal kid and lead a normal life."

"I . . ." Melody shook her head slightly and thrust her hair away from her neck with a nervous gesture. "I don't know what to say, Brand. I . . . you see . . . I'm engaged to be married."

He gave a sardonic grin. "I know. I saw the ring." His voice hardened. "It doesn't alter matters, however. It's either me . . . or Dale. So which is it to be?"

Suddenly, Melody was blazingly furious. How she hated this man who had once been her husband and lover. He had always been hard, a man used to making decisions and having them instantly obeyed, and in that respect he certainly had not changed. And with sudden deep certainty, she knew that his proposal had nothing to do with his younger sister, at least not primarily. No, he was driving this bargain purely from revenge. He held the whip in his hand and he had no hesitation about using it. He wanted to hurt her and the only possible way he could do so now was through her brother.

She glanced again at Dale and saw both the appeal and the blaze of hope in his eyes and knew herself beaten. The hot anger drained away, leaving her empty and cold.

"All right," Melody said huskily, in a voice that sounded strange and foreign to her own ears. "You win, of course."

Chapter Two

One week later, Melody became Mrs. Brand Travers for the second time. They were remarried in one of the numerous wedding chapels in Las Vegas and Melody could not help but compare this wedding to their first one. It had been in a church, complete with flowers, a formal wedding gown, and all their friends and relatives in attendance. This time she wore a flowered pastel-yellow dress, and though there were flowers, the only guest was Dale. But the greatest difference was their own attitudes. The first time they had joined together with overflowing love and joy and an erroneous confidence in their future as man and wife. This time Brand was stony-faced while Melody was numb, and there was no hope at all for their future as far as their personal relationship was concerned. The first time had ended bitterly; the second time was beginning with bitterness.

Curiously, however, the preceding week had not been entirely unpleasant. Once the die had been cast, Brand had softened in his attitude toward Dale. He had insisted that he stay and vacation as planned with Melody . . . and now, of course, himself, and the three of them did everything together. Although Dale did not once gamble again, not even so much as to place a dollar bet on keno or a few nickles in a slot machine, they visited casinos and watched others; they drove out into the mountains one day and enjoyed Nevada's golden, sunny dry air; another day they visited nearby Hoover Dam and Lake Mead, and every evening they attended a different show at one or another of the luxurious hotels along the Strip.

During that week, Brand made no effort whatsoever to be alone with Melody. In fact, he seemed to deliberately avoid any such opportunity whenever it presented itself. His demeanor toward her was almost identical to Dale's—lighthearted and casual—and if it hadn't been for the knowledge that Brand was forcing her to return to a loveless marriage, Melody could have found herself totally enjoying that week.

But now the wedding was over and they were back at the hotel. The two men were in the sitting room of Brand's suite and Melody could hear the murmur of their voices through the door in the bedroom, where she had gone to comb her hair and renew her lipstick.

She glanced around the room and her gaze flashed quickly past the predominant, king-sized bed to her own luggage, which sat near the closet door. She ought to unpack, she thought dully, but for the moment she could not bring herself to do so.

She picked up the comb and turned to the mirror. Her face was sallow. Her eyes were dark and dulled, like her emotions.

She lifted her left hand to smooth her hair into place as she combed it with her right and as she did so she caught a flash of the diamonds there. She again wore the engage-

19

ment and wedding rings she had left behind when she had run away from Brand five years ago. She lowered her hand and stared at them for some time. They seemed to mock her. Right now she was as much a prisoner as Dale would have been had he gone to prison, and yet she had done the only thing possible. She could not watch her own brother go to prison if it were within her power to stop it.

She sighed and, bracing her shoulders, walked across the room to the door.

Champagne had been delivered while she had been in the bedroom. Brand stood beside the table, pouring it into three long-stemmed glasses while Dale spoke over the telephone. Melody sat down on the sofa.

Dale cradled the receiver and said cheerfully, "Well, that's okay. My flight reservation is confirmed for this afternoon."

Brand came and handed Melody a glass of the champagne. Then he handed Dale a glass, picked up his own, and lifted it in a toast. "To our future," he said, and his face was grave as he looked at Melody.

"To your future," Dale echoed in a hearty voice.

Melody slowly raised her glass. The toast was absurd, the celebration a farce, under the circumstances, but what was done was now done and there was no point in being churlish.

After they drank the toast, Brand sat down beside Melody and he stretched out his arm along the top of the sofa behind her. She tensed at once, but when he did not touch her, she gradually relaxed.

"Now you understand exactly what you're to do when you get home?" Brand asked.

Dale nodded his head and ticked off in a brisk manner, "One, visit your grandparents and tell them about the marriage. Two, send a cable to Dad. Three, inform the office and home staff. And fourth, take the next plane to Chicago for that meeting with the Whitaker Company."

"Right. They're a hard-nosed outfit but we're offering

them a good, fair market price and I know you'll bring them around."

Dale drained his glass and stood up. "Well, I'd better get back to my room and finish packing. I won't see you again until you're back at home, so . . . best wishes to the both of you." He came over to Melody and dropped a light kiss on the top of her head. "I know you'll be happy, Mel," he said softly.

Melody could only stare at him. For the life of her, she could not have mustered up a smile. Dale was behaving just as though all this were normal and natural and that he had done nothing at all to ruin her entire life!

When she did not respond, Dale's face reddened slightly and then he turned to his brother-in-law. "Brand, I . . . well, thanks for giving me another chance."

Brand nodded and stood up. "I know you won't let me . . . or Melody . . . down again."

Dale grinned with self-consciousness. "That's a promise," he vowed as they shook hands. "Well, so long." And, quickly, he crossed the floor and went out the door.

This was the moment Melody had been dreading the most, the time when inevitably she and Brand would have to be alone together. She laced her fingers tightly together in her lap and her face was strained as she looked at her husband from across the room.

"It's almost noon," he commented mildly. "Do you want lunch served here in the room or shall we go down to the restaurant?"

"I'd . . . I'd rather go to the restaurant," she answered quickly.

Brand's thick dark brows lifted and there was a faint smile touching his lips. "Reprieve?" His hands went to his waist as he stood watching her. "The time of reckoning between us is inevitable, Melody."

She ignored that and rose to her feet. "I . . . I'll just get my purse," she told him.

They had a leisurely meal and Brand ordered wine to

accompany it. When Melody tried to protest, he shook his head. "I know you don't have much of a capacity for alcohol, but I think you can survive one glass of champagne and an additional glass or two of wine. People don't get married every day, do they?"

"No?" she snapped sarcastically. "We certainly seem to make a habit of it!"

Brand laughed outright at that. "I'm glad to see all your former spirit isn't gone," he said with approval. "This past week I've had my doubts."

"Have you?" she asked dryly. "I'm surprised at you, Brand. I thought the whole purpose of forcing me into this was to crush my spirit."

His frown came, darkly dispelling the smile. "Then you've got it all wrong," he said sharply. "When you first deserted me like you did I was angry enough to crush the very life out of you, but even anger mellows in time." He shook his head. "No, I don't want to crush your spirit. It's one of the things I always admired about you."

Melody felt surprise and even a touch of pleasure at his words, but she carefully concealed it. "Maybe you haven't crushed it," she admitted, "but you've certainly squeezed it a bit."

Brand laughed again. "Maybe I had to, Mrs. Travers," he said as he lifted his glass of wine to his lips. "Maybe I had to."

She eyed him thoughtfully. "Why did you want to marry me again, Brand?"

He looked annoyed at the question. "I told you, because of Tammy."

Melody shook her head. "I don't believe you. Or at least that's not all of it."

"No?" he asked. "Then what do you think is my real purpose?"

Melody shrugged her shoulders. "Revenge," she said quietly.

"Revenge because you ran out on me?" he asked. At

22

her nod, he gazed off across the room for a long moment and then his eyes came to meet hers. "Maybe you're right."

The spirit he had spoken of a few minutes earlier drained away and Melody stared at her plate, her appetite gone. How could two people possibly base a marriage on revenge? It could only end with disastrous results.

The meal was finally over, and as they left the restaurant Brand said, "I'm sure you would like some time alone upstairs to unpack, so I'll just stay down here in the casino for a while. I'll see you later in the room."

She nodded and moved away from him, glad to have this unexpected time alone. Her face felt flushed and slightly feverish and she wondered dully whether she might be coming down with something. But as she punched the elevator button, she remembered the wine. That was why her face felt hot and her eyes were droopy, and with the thought that Brand would be coming up to her later, she suddenly wished she had had more, much more, to drink. Maybe if she learned to drink enough, often enough, she would be able to blot out the sudden turn of events in her life, to blank out the empty future . . . a future with a husband who had once loved her passionately and who now hated her enough to imprison her.

It did not take long to unpack. They would only be staying here a couple more days themselves before returning to Texas . . . only long enough to give Dale time to break the news of their sudden remarriage to everyone and to give the appearance of remaining behind for a short honeymoon.

It felt strange for her to be hanging her clothes in the closet beside Brand's. It had been so long since she had shared a closet . . . or a room . . . or a bed.

She had been avoiding so much as even looking at the bed and its significance, but when she had finished unpacking, the pull of sleepiness overcame her dread of it.

She felt woozy and could scarcely hold her eyes open, even after taking a shower. She wavered for long moments, wondering whether to dress and return downstairs or to try to grab a quick nap, but finally her own uncontrollable yawns made the decision.

She slipped into a soft copper-toned nightgown and crawled between the cool sheets and was almost instantly asleep.

When she awoke, she saw by the bedside clock that it was after four in the afternoon. The shadows in the room had lengthened so that it was almost dark.

Melody stretched and flipped over from her side onto her back, and as she did so was startled to see Brand in the half-gloom, his coat and tie gone, seated in a chair just opposite the bed.

"Did you have a nice rest?" he asked.

"How long have you been sitting there watching me?" she demanded with resentment.

"For the better part of an hour, at least," he admitted readily. "Why does that make you angry? I've certainly seen you sleep often enough—and without any clothes at all!"

Melody's face reddened and she was infuriated with herself because of it. She raised herself up into a sitting position, and as the bedcovers fell away she almost pulled them back but caught herself just in time. After all, Brand was right. He had seen more of her than what the gown revealed times too numerous to mention, so an excess of sensitivity would only serve to make herself appear absurd under the circumstances. Even though she might hate him for forcing her into this situation, where he again had the right to share her bedroom, she was not going to allow him to know the true extent of how much it upset her. Now her chin jutted out with unconscious pride.

"It's not that," she lied. "But it isn't very pleasant to wake up and find someone has been watching you."

Brand rose with the grace of a panther and swiftly

eliminated the distance between them. "Not just anyone, " he reminded her as he sank to the edge of the bed beside her. "Your husband." His hand reached out to brush a strand of her tousled hair away from her forehead.

His nearness shook her. Melody's senses were acutely aware of Brand's compelling masculinity. His dark gaze traveled from her face down to her slender neck and further, to her sensitive throat, and then to the swell of her breasts, and as it did, she could feel heat rising in her face and in her racing blood.

"You're even more beautiful now than you were five years ago," he told her softly just before he lowered his head and his lips claimed hers.

His hands went to her shoulders and gently they pulled her forward until her breasts were touching his chest. Fire streaked through her as his lips forced hers to open and respond, though Melody tried vainly to remain unaffected.

At last he raised his head and now his hand stroked her throat in a light, sensual touch that seemed somehow to affect her breathing processes, and as the hand dropped to cup her breast, Melody shook her head slowly from side to side.

"Brand, please . . . no . . ." She murmured weakly, even as desire began to clamor through her veins.

"Don't be silly," he told her huskily. "We never could resist each other physically and you know it." His hands left her as he began to unbutton his shirt.

Melody closed her eyes in defeat as Brand undressed and got into the bed beside her. He would have his way, she knew, and then her carefully built defenses over these past five years would crumble into dust. For though she had carefully schooled her mind to forget Brand, her heart and her body had not.

A moment later he took her into his strong arms, and as his long, lean body pressed against the soft pliance of hers, she was lost. Passions that she had long denied existence ignited into life, engulfing her like a raging inferno. All thought was banished and there was only this blaze that flared between them, consuming them utterly.

When at last, drained and spent, they lay slightly apart, Brand turned his head against the pillow to glance at her. "You enjoyed that." he stated flatly.

Melody stared at the ceiling, avoiding his eyes. "Yes," she agreed unwillingly. How could she deny it when every part of her body had shamelessly acknowledged it?

"There was never anything wrong between us in bed," he pursued, and now his voice was hard, tinged with anger. "So what was it, Melody? Why did you run away from me like you did?"

Melody shook her head. "I don't care to discuss it," she told him.

"Damn it," Brand exploded, "Don't you think you owe me an explanation? You were my *wife!*"

"I owe you nothing," she responded in a raspy voice. "Nothing! And the fact that you've forced me to marry you again doesn't alter what went before." Heedless of her nudity, Melody left the bed and headed for the bathroom.

She took a second shower, this time trying to scrub away her anger at both herself and Brand. Her treacherous body had betrayed logic and had responded to his lovemaking with the same weakness it had had when they had been married the first time. Brand had said there had never been anything wrong between them in bed, and she had thought at one time that that was true. But it could not have been true, because if it had, why had he been unfaithful to her?

Was Lorraine White still Brand's secretary? she wondered. And why had he not married her after their divorce?

Melody chewed at her bottom lip as the hot water splayed across her body. The very thought of Lorraine still had the power to put a bitter lump in the pit of her stomach. Lorraine had given her a difficult time from the day she had married Brand, deliberately attacking the shy, insecure eighteen-year-old she had been, doing all she could to subtly make her feel even more out of her depth than she felt already. Brand's social prominence and great wealth had been a hard enough hurdle for her to jump, and Lorraine had made it more so at every turn, always pointing out her inadequacies.

She had coped, though, for two years, because of her love for Brand. She had been careful to conceal her fear of Lorraine from him as well as her other insecurities and had done her best to grow and learn to fit into his world. And it had seemed all right, as far as their personal relationship with each other was concerned.

Even so, she had always sensed a competition between herself and Lorraine. Brand made no secret of the fact that he liked and admired her, both as a secretary and as a woman. But it was not until that one particular business trip he and Dale had taken to Los Angeles that she had learned the truth . . . that Brand and Lorraine were actually sleeping together.

Now she turned off the taps and stepped out of the shower. She dried herself roughly as her thoughts pursued their own course. Brand had needed some papers from the office pertaining to that business trip and he had had Lorraine fly out and join them. There had been no secret about that. In fact, she told herself grimly, there had been no attempt at secrecy whatsoever.

The memory of it rose up to taunt her. Brand had been in the habit of telephoning her almost every night whenever he had been out of town, but on that particular evening Melody had tried to call him. She had been lonely and missing him and had only wanted to hear his voice. But there had been no answer to her calls earlier in the evening, and finally, just as she was about to go to bed at midnight, she decided to try to call him once more.

And Lorraine, not Brand, had answered the telephone

in his hotel room! It had been such a shock she had not been able to speak, and an instant later Brand's voice had come over the wire and it had sounded thick with sleepiness.

Melody had hung up the phone without speaking. There had been nothing she could say . . . then or now. The hurt had sliced so deeply it was a cut that would never heal, though five years had dulled its sharp pain. But even after this much time had elapsed, she could not bring herself to mention it face to face to Brand. She supposed it was her own pride's defense. It was shaming and degrading and not once in the past five years had she ever mentioned what had happened to anyone. She had done the only thing she had known to do at the time . . . run.

And until now she hadn't done so badly. Little by little, she had rebuilt her life and discovered that though it perhaps lacked something, nevertheless she could live without Brand. She had been gone before he returned from that trip and for two months had not even telephoned Dale to let him know where she was. She had first needed to get a grip over her own emotions. But she finally contacted him, and immediately afterward Brand had telephoned her, his voice over the wire like frigid ice water, and he had not argued when she had informed him that she wanted a divorce.

She smiled without amusement as she thought of the lawyer who had handled her divorce. He had clearly believed she was crazy for not trying to get a large property settlement from Brand, but she had wanted nothing and had refused anything except enough money for her support while she attended secretarial school. And once she had found a job with another lawyer, Rob Willis, she had written Brand a polite note asking him to stop sending money, which he had promptly done. And not once in all that time had he tried to see her, which was what made all this so incomprehensible now . . . his sudden demand that she marry him once more.

With a sigh, she shrugged into her robe and went out into the bedroom.

Two days later, they left Las Vegas. As the plane carried them east over Hoover Dam and, a short time later, across the gigantic chasm of the Grand Canyon, Melody paid little heed. She was quietly facing the fact that she was now on her way back to the life she had once abandoned and that this time there was no joy to look forward to as she once had. Though Brand might act as loverlike as before whenever they were in bed, there was a hard streak to him now that was new and unfamiliar and it made him a stranger.

In Dallas they took a taxi to Melody's apartment so that she could pack a few more clothes and make arrangements to have the remainder of her belongings sent on later by trunk.

Brand left her going through her closet while he went down to speak to the apartment manager for her. The instant he was gone, Melody dropped what she was doing and rushed to the telephone to call Rob. Dale had promised to call him and tell him about her marriage, but even so, she owed him a personal explanation, and this was the first time she had been away from Brand long enough to do so.

Rob was furious with her. "How in hell could you do this to me?" he demanded angrily "You leave me in the lurch for a secretary besides just suddenly dumping our wedding plans. I thought you loved me."

Melody licked her dry lips. "I . . . I know it seems dreadful of me, Rob," she conceded, "but it . . . well, it's not all very straightforward."

"What do you mean?" he asked.

"I . . . I can't explain, but truly, when I left here to meet Dale I had no intention of seeing Brand or . . . or of marrying him again."

There was a long, cold silence and then Rob demanded,

"Are you telling me you were coerced into marrying the guy again?"

Exactly, Melody thought. But of course she could not possibly say it. "No, of course not," she denied quickly. "It . . . it just happened suddenly. That's all I meant. I'm truly sorry, Rob. I didn't mean to hurt you. I never wanted to hurt you and I . . ."

The bedroom door suddenly banged against the wall. Melody, seated on the edge of the bed, whirled around and went white as she saw Brand standing there glowering at her.

"How touching," he sneered, and his face was dark with displeasure. "Tell lover boy he'll receive his engagement ring back by registered mail."

"I . . ." Melody dully repeated what Brand told her to say and then she added in a lower voice, "I've got to hang up now, Rob. I . . . I'll write you and . . . and explain further. I'm sorry. Good-bye."

As she hung up the phone, Brand strode across the room and with startling violence jerked her roughly to her feet. "I'd better not find out that you ever contact him in any way whatsoever," he threatened through gritted teeth. "No letters or phone calls or visits. Is that clear?"

"You can't stop me!" she hissed defiantly as she twisted her arm vainly in his tight grasp.

"I can," he countered with dangerous coldness, "and if I ever discover that you try to cheat on me, I'll make you sorry you were ever born, and that's a promise."

Melody's eyes widened with astonishment and hurt fury singed her words. "What's all right for you isn't all right for me, is that it?" she gasped. "Rules don't apply to you?"

Brand frowned and he dropped her arm. As she began to nurse it, he demanded, "What the devil are you talking about?"

Melody shook her head. In the heat of the moment she had already said more than she had meant to. Brand was

30

putting on a cool act of innocence and lack of understanding, all of which was a lie, but even now, under attack herself, she had no desire to discuss his tawdry affair with Lorraine. It was in the past and there she wanted to leave it, but the future was a different matter.

"Let's get this straight between us right now, Brand," she said with a hint of steel in her voice that matched his own. "If my romances with other men must be over, then yours with other women had better be, too. No matter what the circumstances of our marriage this time, I will not be made a laughing stock for others."

To her surprise, Brand nodded and agreed. "We will base this marriage on fidelity, regardless of our personal emotions or feelings toward each other. I believe we should be able to expect that, at least, from one another."

He was lying, of course, Melody thought. Brand didn't stick to the rules of fidelity the first time, when he was supposedly in love with her, so there was scant reason to believe he would do so now. But it had been a long, tiring day and she did not have the energy or the desire to argue the point.

Dispiritedly, she turned and resumed the chore of packing her clothes.

Chapter Three

They stayed the night in Melody's apartment and the next morning they returned again to the huge Dallas airport for the last leg of their journey.

Melody was tense on the plane as she thumbed through the airline's magazine. She stared at the pages with blank eyes, her thoughts too much in a jumble to allow her to concentrate on the articles. She was wondering how she would be received once they arrived. She had had a close relationship with Brand's grandparents and his young sister, but that had been before she had run away, and

31

they were bound to feel differently about her now. Brand's friends, too. No one knew why she had left him, and everyone was bound to have come to their own conclusions and found her wanting. It was bad enough knowing she now had to live again with this man who sat quietly beside her, but she also had to live in his world, facing his friends and his family, and Melody did not deceive herself for one instant that it was going to be easy.

The flight seemed incredibly short. Melody supposed it was because she had been so engrossed in her worries. She turned to glance at Brand, who was just waking up. He had napped during the trip, causing her to envy him his total ease. Whatever was ahead of them, it clearly did not bother him as it did her, and for a moment she even hated him for that. He could bring her back and pluck her down into the middle of a highly uncomfortable situation and it did not so much as cause him a single moment's unrest.

But then, why should it? she chided herself. Hadn't he married her again just for revenge? And if that were true, then he must actually be taking a pleasure in knowing that she was nervous and filled with misgivings.

Brand stretched his long legs as far as the tight space would allow. "Ah, it'll be good to get home," he murmured.

Melody did not answer, and a second later she felt the force of Brand's keen gaze on her as she turned her head to look out the window. Below was Nueces Bay and, as the plane descended for its landing, she could spot several boats on the water. Then she saw the arc of the harbor bridge over the channel and the huge tankers that were docked in the port.

A moment later the plane was making the horrible screaming noise of descent. Melody always hated this moment of flying and she squeezed her eyes tightly shut and clutched the armrests with her fingers. Brand's hand came out to cover hers and she opened her eyes and blinked at him in surprise. The plane was down now, taxiing along the runway, but Melody was aware only of Brand's dark eyes upon her. Her heart began to thud erratically. She was mesmerized by the expression his gaze held. There was a solemn significance in it that she could not quite identify.

"It's going to work, Melody," he said in a low, compelling voice. "The past is past, but our future together is going to work." Wordlessly, she nodded, and it evoked an approving smile to his lips. "Good girl," he said lightly as he withdrew his hand.

As soon as they left the plane, the warm, humid air and the strong Gulf wind assaulted them. Melody's skirt began flapping wildly against her legs and her hair lifted from her neck and whipped in all directions. She was carrying her overnight bag as well as her purse and it was a struggle to hold the skirt in place, impossible to do the same for her hair. Brand happened to glance down at her, saw her plight, and began to laugh.

Melody laughed, too, and realized as she did that it was the first spontaneous laughter they had shared since they had first seen each other over a week ago. The release it offered made her feel suddenly lighthearted and almost happy.

"About to get blown away?" he asked as he took her overnight case from her hand so that she could better manage her wayward skirt.

"I'd forgotten Corpus Christi's winds," she acknowledged. "Not to mention the humidity. I feel sticky already."

"Give you a week and you won't notice either," Brand prophesied.

"I know," she agreed. "When I first went to Dallas I felt stifled without that constant breeze, and I still miss the water. The first thing I plan to do is spend some time on the patio and get a tan."

Brand grinned. "Seems like we've still got a few things here that appeal to you, after all. And I'm looking forward to the appealing picture you'll make . . . in your bikini!" The last he had added in a low, teasing voice as he leaned toward her ear so that others couldn't hear.

Melody wrinkled her nose at him, not dignifying the comment with an answer. They were walking behind other deplaning passengers along the long, open-aired corridor toward the main terminal building. There was a sudden part in the crowd and a tall woman several yards away saw them and waved beckoningly.

"Brand! Over here, Brand!"

Melody felt a sick twinge in her stomach. The pleasant mood of only moments ago evaporated. As they drew level with the other woman, Melody's spine stiffened and her shoulders tensed.

"Hello, Lorraine." Brand smiled. "I didn't expect to see you out here."

Lorraine White returned the smile and Melody noted that she was still as beautiful as ever. Her smooth ash-blond hair was swept back away from her face into a sleek, businesslike arrangement that was nevertheless artfully charming, and somehow the gusty winds did not seem to dare to displace one single strand of it. She wore a beige two-piece business suit with a burnt-orange scarf at the neck that aided her air of sophisticated efficiency. Melody at once reverted to the self-conscious awareness of her old inadequacies and she knotted her hands at her sides as Lorraine spoke in a low, almost intimate voice to Brand, deliberately attempting to exclude her.

"I decided to come out and pick you up myself," Lorraine explained to him, "instead of having one of the men from the office do it. It's been very lonely without you. Did you have a good trip?"

"A very good trip," Brand answered in a relaxed manner. "It was considerate of you to come, Lorraine, although we could have taken a cab."

"Of course," Lorraine agreed, "but I thought this way I could fill you in on business news while we drive." Only now did she at last allow her gaze to acknowledge Melody's presence. The steel-gray eyes were cold and unwelcoming as she said, "Hello, Melody. Dale told me you'd be coming."

There was no answer to that since there was no pleasantry involved, so Melody contented herself with an equally brief, "Hello, Lorraine."

"Let's get our bags," Brand suggested. "I'm sure Melody's anxious to get home and get unpacked."

Lorraine's eyes narrowed at that, but she did not have a chance to respond because Brand was urging them both forward toward the doors at the end of the corridor.

The drive from the airport into the city was accomplished in total silence for Melody, and she understood at once why Lorraine had come to chauffeur them. It was her car, and it seemed only natural for Brand to sit in the front seat beside her while they discussed business matters. That left Melody to occupy the back seat alone, shut out both physically and conversationally. Lorraine was telling her at once, without a word, that she would always outmaneuver her.

But somehow, despite the bitterness of the past, it did not bother Melody as it once would have done. This time her emotions were not involved. True, she was Brand's wife again, but this time she did not love him. She had paid a dear price before she had finally gotten over that love and now she had no intentions of ever allowing her innermost spirit to be affected again by either of them.

The city had grown enormously during the years she had been absent, and Melody gazed about her with interest. It was a beautiful day with an almost cloudless blue sky above and the buildings they passed were whitewashed by the bright sunlight.

They took the southern route on the freeway toward Padre Island at Brand's direction, so that Melody could see how much that area had built up. South Padre Island Drive, which five years ago had still been chiefly large blocks of farming land interspersed with a few small shopping areas, now was clogged with new businesses, new shopping centers and banks, and a corresponding increase in traffic.

At Airline, Lorraine left the freeway and turned the car toward the bay and Melody felt a quiver of excitement race through her. In a few minutes they would be home.

Home! The word struck her as incongruous under the circumstances. And yet the excitement and anticipation refused to die. Her heart knew the truth. She *was* coming home, after a long, self-imposed exile.

They reached Ocean Drive, along which were some of the most magnificent homes in the city. Oleanders flowered, white and pink, bougainvilleas bloomed riotously, and palm tree fronds fluttered and waved in the tangy sea breeze. But Melody's eyes were on the bay. It was a sparkling, aquamarine blue today and in the distance she could see several sailboats soaring along as though they had wings.

Lorraine turned the car off the street, driving between tall white gateposts, and then swept around the curve, coming to a halt before the pillared entrance.

As Melody stepped out of the car, she gazed up at the house with appreciation. It was two-storied, glistening white with neat, black shutters guarding the windows. The red-stoned entrance porch was graced with heavy urns from which tall, round-sculptured shrubs thrust upward and along the front of the house were neat flower beds, rampant with vividly colored flowers. The small front lawn was shady with trees and beyond, near the fence, were thick borders of oleanders, which screened the house from the busy street. Nothing, outside at least, had changed, and Melody sighed with satisfaction.

Brand unloaded their bags from the car and the three of them mounted the steps and went inside the house into the cool hall.

"I took the liberty of making you an appointment for a

business luncheon, Brand," Lorraine said, as he dropped the bags and walked over to a side table, picked up a stack of mail, and began shuffling through it.

He frowned swiftly. "Why did you do that?" he demanded. "I'm tired and I had planned on spending the rest of the day at home with Melody."

"I understand that," Lorraine said soothingly, "but it's Mr. Wickers and he simply insisted on seeing you today as soon as you returned. You see, he's leaving on a trip himself tomorrow."

Brand sighed and ran his hand through his hair as he turned to look at Melody with an apology in his eyes. "I suppose I'll have to go, then," he acknowledged. "Will you be all right?"

"Why on earth shouldn't she be all right?" Lorraine asked irritably. "It's not as if the house is strange to her." She tapped an impatient foot against the blue Mexican-tiled floor.

"I'll be absolutely fine, Brand," Melody said quickly. "You go ahead and attend to your business."

"And what will you do?" he asked.

She shrugged her shoulders. "I'll unpack first, and then perhaps I'll spend the afternoon sunbathing."

There was a sudden teasing sparkle in his eyes and they were both remembering the comment he had made at the airport, but before he could say anything, Lorraine said, "It's really getting late, Brand. We'd better go if you want to make the luncheon on time."

Brand nodded and withdrew his gaze from Melody. "Right."

"You'll come with me?"

He turned to look at her in surprise. "Then how would I get to the restaurant?" he asked. "I'll take my own car. I'll meet you at the office in half an hour."

It was clearly a dismissal, and Melody saw Lorraine force a tight little smile to her lips before she nodded. "All right, see you then."

After she was gone, Brand apologized again. "I really am sorry, Melody. Your first day back."

She smiled at him, and was amazed at the gladness in her heart that he had truly wanted to stay with her. For some reason, it mattered quite a lot. "It's all right," she said again. "Truly. I'll keep busy."

Just then a housemaid came along the hall and expressed surprise at seeing them standing there. Brand smiled at her. "This is Mrs. Travers, Opal. I have to go out, but I'd appreciate it if you would get Barney in to carry our luggage upstairs and then if you would help my wife unpack."

Opal smiled. "Certainly, Mr. Travers. It's nice to have you back. I'll tell Juanita that Mrs. Travers will be needing some lunch." She turned and left them.

Brand walked toward the front door, paused, then turned and came back. With the swiftness of a seagull dipping for its food, he bent his head, kissed her lips lightly and then was gone.

Melody stood still for several minutes, her fingers touching her lips, then she shook her head and went slowly toward the stairs.

The rest of the day passed swiftly. Melody spent most of the morning unpacking both hers and Brand's clothes, politely spurning Opal's help.

She had been surprised to discover that Brand's bedroom . . . *their* bedroom . . . had undergone no change whatsoever. It was a large, spacious room overlooking the bay and it was done in cool shades of sea greens and blues with complementary furnishings of white bamboo and accented with lush, tropical green plants. She had decorated it herself, loving the sea so much she had wanted to bring its soothing influence into the house with them, and Brand had indulgently given her her way. It had been so intimately their room, with the stamp of her own personality upon it, that she had not expected to find it still the same, but she was glad that it was. It seemed to

38

offer a welcome to her, blunting the edge of the strangeness of her return.

At noon she went down the circular staircase and into the small breakfast room just behind the formal dining room. Juanita brought in her lunch, a cool shrimp salad with fruit and cheese on the side.

Melody smiled at her diffidently, unsure of her reception. Nobody knew exactly how old Juanita was, with her grayed hair and the fine network of wrinkles that creased her browned face, but though her movements were slow and sometimes painful because of arthritis, she was a force to be reckoned with. She had been a part of the Travers household since before Brand had ever been born, and though by rights she should have been able to relax and have others wait upon her in her golden years, she obstinately refused to do so. Her opinions mattered and carried weight in the Travers household, from Brand right down to the housemaid, and no one was exempt from the sharpness of her tongue if she felt they deserved it. Melody had been favored in the past and rarely subjected to the barbed-wire prick of her words, but now her luck had run out.

Juanita stood, hands on ample hips, and cocked her head to the side as she openly studied Melody. "You're even scrawnier than you were before," she said critically.

"Hello, Juanita," Melody said. "How are you?"

"I am fine," the old lady acknowledged grudgingly. "So . . . you've come back," she added in a flat voice.

"Y-yes." Melody managed another tentative smile. "I've come back."

"Humph! And how long do you intend to stay around this time?"

"Juanita!" Melody's voice was a plea. "I . . . look, there were reasons why I left and . . ."

Juanita nodded. "*Sí*, I should hope so after the uproar you caused us all."

All at once Melody realized that the old woman had

39

been personally hurt over her abrupt departure. Juanita had been fond of her, taking Melody to her large, generous heart just as she had loved Brand and Tammy, and she felt Melody had let her down as well as Brand.

Melody pushed back her chair and rose to her feet. "I'm sorry, Juanita," she said softly. "I had to go . . . but now I'm back, and I've missed you very much!"

"Humph," Juanita sniffed again but as Melody wrapped her arms around her shoulders, her own arms came out to encircle Melody's waist, and there was a tiny smile to her withered lips when they drew apart. Then she gave Melody a tiny shove and said, "Eat your lunch."

Obediently, Melody sat down again and picked up her fork. "Tell me about Tammy and Gram and Gramps, and your own family," she said. "How is everyone?"

Juanita shrugged her shoulders. "Mr. and Mrs. Travers, they're like me. Age is touching them, but they get along. My children are fine. I have seven grandchildren now."

"And Tammy?" Melody asked before she took a bite of the delicious salad.

Juanita shook her head. "She's not the same sweet child she used to be. Now she is always sullen and angry. She don't listen to what old Juanita says anymore, or to anyone else, either. I think it's those schools that did it. She hated them, but still, what could Mr. Travers do? He couldn't raise her alone and I must be in my own home at night. And the grandparents are too old. She's with them now, you know, but it is not good for any of them if she stays too long. Things aren't restful when Tammy is around."

Melody did not miss the hint of accusation in Juanita's words. It was as though she were blaming her, Melody, for the change in Tammy's personality. She sighed and her appetite for lunch vanished. Brand had told her he needed help with Tammy, but he had not told her that his sister had become difficult, except for the fact that she hated the boarding schools. Melody only hoped that it was all in

Juanita's imagination. After all, Tammy was a teenager now . . . a fifteen-year-old . . . and she could be expected to exert a certain amount of independence from authority, and perhaps Juanita was just too old to have the necessary patience needed for dealing with the girl. At least she hoped that was all it was.

Late that afternoon, Melody sat on the patio in the cool shade cast by the house and the surrounding trees. She sipped at her iced lemonade and gazed idly at the gray-green waters of the bay. She had showered and changed into a white sundress and now she lay back in the lounge chair and relaxed, enjoying the sensuous touch of the sea breeze on her skin. Down at the foot of the bluff was the shoreline and a fishing pier that protruded out into the water. Several sea gulls were flapping over the pier, searching, as ever, for food. Melody toyed with the idea of carrying some bread crumbs down to toss to them, but she felt too lazy and comfortable to move.

During the hot part of the afternoon, she had gone for a swim in the pool that was at one side of the house but which could not be seen from where she now sat. It had been cool and refreshing, but it had been a rather lonely swim. Memories of other times, when Brand had been with her, had come unbidden to her mind, disturbing and taunting, and it had not been long before she had climbed out.

That was the problem with the entire house, she thought unhappily as she closed her eyes. Every room evoked memories of happier times, and though one part of her was delighted to become reacquainted with the house, another part of her was tortured. The bedroom especially, in spite of its welcoming appeal, had affected her senses, causing an unreasonable pain that she did not know how to heal.

"Here she is," Brand's voice intruded into her thoughts. "I brought a couple of dinner guests along, Melody."

She sat upright in the chair. Brand was stepping from the hall out onto the flagstoned patio and behind him were Dale and Lorraine.

"How . . . how pleasant," she managed to get out. "I'll go in at once and tell Juanita." As she started to rise, Brand reached down a hand to her arm and helped her up.

Dale came and kissed her cheek. "Hi, sis. How's the honeymoon?"

Melody looked at him with sober eyes and his face flushed beneath her unwavering gaze. He backed away from her with a quick movement and said heartily, "I sure could use a drink, Brand."

"Of course," Brand said politely. Then he turned to Lorraine. "What would you like?"

"The usual," Lorraine said in a silken voice. "You know exactly how I like it."

Melody escaped into the house. She informed Juanita to set two more places at the dining table and then she went into the living room to be alone for a few minutes and get a grip on herself. Why had Brand invited Dale and Lorraine for dinnner on their first night at home? Was it to show her at once how it would be . . . that Lorraine was still very much in the scene despite this marriage? It seemed probable and she supposed that Dale had been invited also just to even the number as well as to be someone to distract her attention while Brand paid court to Lorraine.

And that was exactly it, she decided, when she returned to the patio. Dale was sitting beside the patio table, drink in hand, while Lorraine and Brent were a short distance away, ostensibly admiring the roses, but deep in a low-voiced intimate conversation. A moment later, they moved out of sight, going around the house toward the pool.

Melody dropped down into the chair beside her brother as she watched the others vanish behind a thick screen of shrubbery. When she brought her gaze back to him at last,

42

he was eyeing her intently. "I'm sorry, Mel," he said and there was an overlay of bitterness coating his voice that she had never heard before. "I've been telling myself everything was just fine . . . that you'd come around and actually thank me for being the cause of your marrying Brand again, but the truth is, I wrecked everything for you, didn't I?"

She smiled wanly at him. "I can't pretend this is what I wanted, Dale, because it isn't. But if it saved you from prison and from hurting Dad, then it's worth it. Anything is."

Dale smiled and reached out to cover her hand with his. "You're a sister in a million, Mel," he said huskily. "And somehow, someday, I'm going to make it all up to you. I'm saving money now to pay Brand back. I'm even going to find myself a cheaper apartment, and once I've got him paid off, I'll talk to him about releasing you from the deal. I know by then it'll be too late for you and Wallis, but at least you'd be free to live your own life again."

Somehow Melody had a deep inner conviction that it would never happen like that, but she did not say so. Instead she asked him about the business trip to Chicago and he told her it had been a success.

Dinner was not a success, as far as Melody was concerned. The other three talked business almost exclusively and she felt totally alienated. Lorraine did it deliberately, she was certain, and she even suspected Dale of the same. Since their conversation on the patio, he had begun to ignore her, and whenever he happened to glance at her, he seemed ill-at-ease and even embarrassed. It was as though now that she had done what she could for him and he had shown his gratitude, he was uncomfortable with her, perhaps because of the position in which his actions had placed her. Only Brand seemed occasionally to recall that she was at the table too and would make an effort to include her in the conversation.

The scope of the table talk covered several states, at

least one foreign country, and rather huge sums of money. Brand's business interests were diversified and broad, jumping from large blocks of real estate to oil and gas interests to even a couple of small manufacturing plants. His father had been an entrepreneur, parlaying *his* father's cattle money into various other investments until it had grown rapidly, and under Brand's capable hands the Travers holdings had increased even more. There was very little that Brand could not buy with his money, Melody thought bitterly as she toyed with her food, and she, just like his other possessions, had been bought.

Dinner was over at last and the four of them had coffee in the living room, which had an atmosphere of comfortable hominess with its rust-colored sofas and draperies and richly polished golden, natural wood furnishings.

Now the business conversation was forsaken and the talk turned to sports. Lorraine mentioned a golf tournament in which she had recently played and Dale topped her story with a sad tale of his own last golf game, causing them all to laugh.

"When's the last time you got in some fishing?" Brand asked him.

"Not for quite some time," Dale answered. "Now that Mel is back, though, maybe she'll go with me sometime soon. She used to be my lucky charm. I could always catch fish when she was along."

Brand's speculative gaze went to Melody and he smiled. "Yes," he agreed slowly. "She was my lucky charm on fishing trips, too." He rose to his feet. "That reminds me, Dale. I bought a new rod and reel not long ago. Come on out to the storeroom and tell me what you think of it."

The minute the two men were gone, Lorraine leaned forward in her chair, with no trace of the smile on her face that had been there a minute earlier. "Brand may call you his lucky charm," she said in a harsh, menacing voice, "and he may have married you again, but it failed once

44

and it will fail again. And when it does, I'll still be here to pick up the pieces. You were a little fool to come back here. You never did fit in."

Once Lorraine's spiteful words would have reduced Melody to quivering gelatin, but now she was unmoved. Perhaps it was because this time she did not love Brand or perhaps it was because she was more mature. Whatever the cause, her gaze was steady as she returned Lorraine's bold stare.

"Why didn't you bring Brand to the point of asking you to marry him while I was out of the picture, then?" she asked curiously. "After all, Lorraine, you had five years."

Lorraine's lovely features reddened and her mouth tightened with anger. And for one instant there was uncertainty and confusion in her eyes. But then she said forcefully, "I could have, believe me, but I don't want marriage. I value my independence too much for that. Brand and I understand each other, and I think it only fair to warn you now that no wife is going to interfere with our relationship."

A tiny smile played across Melody's lips as she answered quite cheerfully, "But I wouldn't dream of trying, Lorraine. You don't have anything *I'd* want!"

Her self-confident, matter-of-fact demeanor, she noted with quiet satisfaction, had shaken the other woman. There was a bewildered expression in Lorraine's eyes, and before she could frame a retort, the ugly little scene was over. The two men returned to the room and Melody was aware that she had come out the winner because Lorraine turned white at the sight of Brand. She was probably worried about whether or not he had overheard them.

But the victory was hollow. Although she smiled and carried on in the general conversation that followed, Melody wondered bleakly why Brand had bothered to make her marry him again. He could have solved the problem of Tammy a different way and then he would have been free to carry on his affair with his secretary unhampered by the presence of a wife. He had promised fidelity, but if he kept it, surely he was paying a high price just for the sake of revenge!

Chapter Four

Melody awakened abruptly, aware that she was cold. As she reached toward the foot of the bed for the covers, she realized why. She was naked. Her nightgown was a crumpled white heap on the aqua-carpeted floor beside the bed and apparently, while turning in her sleep, she had kicked away the covers.

The other side of the bed was empty, and as she pulled the covers back over her body she could hear the shower running in the adjoining bathroom.

She shivered, but this time it was not from the chill of the air-conditioned room. It was because the memory of the night before had returned.

She had come upstairs to bed just as Dale and Lorraine had departed, and when Brand came a half hour later, she had feigned sleep. It had done her no good.

As soon as he had gotten into bed beside her, his arms had gone around her and his kisses began to explore her sensitive throat as his hands started to caress her.

"I know you aren't asleep," he had whispered, "so stop pretending."

"Leave me alone," she had snapped harshly. "I'm tired tonight."

"Then that's just too bad," he had answered in a hard, unyielding voice, "because I intend to make love to my wife."

"Why don't you just go to Lorraine?" she wanted to scream to him, but prudence stopped her short of actually saying the words. Nothing, however, could stop her from fighting him. He had spent much of the evening ignoring her while he had paid attention to his secretary, so why

46

should he want her now? She was certain he was doing it only out of spite, just to remind her once more that this time he had bought her for a price, and as a result he owned her completely.

Now her heart fluttered anxiously as she recalled the long scratches her nails had dug into his back, of the black fury it had caused and of the ultimate harsh way he had made love to her. *Love*! Her throat choked over the word. It had been an assault that had borne not the slightest bit of relationship to love, and when it had been over she had lain awake for hours, staring dry-eyed at the ceiling, her unhappiness too deep for mere tears as she contemplated an endless future without even the least vestige of tenderness. She might have saved her brother from a prison sentence, but her own was going to be much more difficult to serve.

The spray of water in the shower stopped and the sudden silence reminded Melody that Brand was still close by and that she was still naked. She leaped from the bed, ignoring the crumpled nightgown on the floor and grabbed her robe, wrapping it securely about her and knotting the belt tightly at the waist.

She was standing at the window, gazing down at the bay, when the bathroom door opened. She turned slowly and found Brand's dark, compelling eyes trained on her. His jet-black hair glistened, wet from the shower, and only the lower half of him was covered by a huge thick towel that was wrapped around his waist. His chest and shoulders gleamed in the bright morning light that filled the room.

"So, you're awake," he stated flatly.

"Yes."

"Then get dressed," he ordered. "We'll drive to Rockport this morning and pick up Tammy."

Her spirit rebelled at the commanding tone of his voice, but after last night she was half afraid to cross him. "All right," she said dully. "I won't be long."

As she moved away from the window, about to go into

47

the bathroom, Brand turned his back to her and opened a bureau drawer, and as he did the long red scratches she had put there last night were starkly visible. Melody licked her dry lips and said, "Let me put something on your back."

"Forget it," he said harshly. "I don't need *you* to play nurse."

"I . . . I'm sorry," she said contritely as she moved closer to have a better look. "I . . . I know you're angry with me but you'll have to let me tend to those scratches all the same. Otherwise they might get infected."

"I said forget it," he snapped angrily as he turned to glare at her.

Melody flinched beneath the dark fury in his eyes and without a word went into the bathroom. A moment later she was back with hydrogen peroxide, cotton balls, and some antiseptic ointment.

"Sit on the edge of the bed," she ordered to his taut back.

Brand turned slowly and for a long moment it was an impasse, but she did not withdraw her gaze from him, and finally he flung himself face down across the bed in a violent movement. "Get on with it, then," he growled.

She sat down beside him and winced herself as she applied the liquid to the scratch marks, but outside of a small, involuntary flexing of his muscles, Brand remained motionless.

When she was able to run ointment into the wounds, she did so gently, and despite the horror of last night her fingers began to find sensuous pleasure as they fluttered across the sinewy muscles of his back.

Abruptly, Brand sat upright so that her hands were forced to fall to her lap. "That's enough," he said.

Wordlessly, she looked at him, and finally nodded and rose. Why was he so furious with her, she wondered. Was it only because she had scratched him or was there something more? Surely she had the greater right to be angry after the way he had forced her to submit to him last

48

night, and yet just now, as she had touched him, she had felt her own anger beginning to drain away.

With a sigh, she went into the bathroom for her shower. There was no question, she thought despondently as she closed the door, that Brand was an entirely different person from the man she had once known. Now he was a total stranger to her.

It was another beautiful summer day as they drove away from the house in Brand's cream-colored Chrysler. The islands in the center of Ocean Drive were eye-catching with their lavish display of flowers and swaying palms. Corpus Christi Bay was sparkling beneath the brilliant sun and cloudless sky.

They drove past the L and T heads, where numerous boats were moored, and Melody asked, "Do you still have *The Tammy*?"

"Not the same one," Brand said. "Now we've got *The Tammy II*."

Melody gazed wistfully toward the cluster of boats, boats of all sizes and shapes, from small pleasure crafts to large deep-sea fishing charter boats. She had always enjoyed sailing with Brand, but judging from the forbidding set of his jaw, it was doubtful whether he would ever invite her again. She wondered whether he, like she, was recalling lazy days they had spent together on the sailboat, days when they had been so much in love with each other that they had treasured those brief escapes from the demands and daily pressures of the rest of the world.

She shook her head slightly as though by doing something physical she could dispel the torturing memories. She did not want to remember those days. They were gone forever and so was her innocent belief in love.

They crossed the harbor bridge and, glancing down, Melody could see several large ships. They came from around the world, handling such cargoes as oil, grains, and cotton.

A few minutes later they were on the Nueces Bay

Causeway and Brand reached into his pocket and extracted a cigarette. "Light it for me," he said.

Melody took the cigarette and lit it, then handed it back to him, resenting the fact that he had asked her to perform the little service. It was something she had always done for him whenever they drove together, only in the past she had considered it a pleasant, intimate act.

"Thanks," he said carelessly. He glanced across at her briefly before returning his attention to his driving. "When we get there, I expect you to play the part of the loving wife."

She was startled, and now she frowned thoughtfully. "That might be a little difficult," she told him.

His mouth tightened. "Maybe so," he answered, "but still, I expect you to carry it off. Gram and Gramps are getting old and they're not in the best of health. I don't intend to have them upset or worried about our marriage in any way."

Melody stared down at her hands, which were clenched in her lap. "All right," she agreed. "I'll do my best. I don't want to upset them any more than you do. I love them, too. But, Brand . . ." Suddenly she turned to look at him, "We can't hide the way we feel about each other forever, you know. They're bound to find out sometime. Gran is a very astute person."

"They had better not ever find out," Brand said roughly. "Or anyone else, either. Get this straight, Melody—we're married again for good, so there's no point in causing any more talk about us than there'll already be over the fact of our remarriage. Dale knows the truth, but I damn well don't intend anyone else to know."

She wondered why he did not mention Lorraine. The assured way the other woman had attacked her last evening seemed to prove that she knew the truth as well. And so would others, soon enough, she felt sure. After all, if Brand had been having an affair with Lorraine all these years it couldn't be quite the deep secret he

50

supposed. People weren't blind to things like that, especially when they went on endlessly. And what of the future? In Dallas they had made a bargain to be faithful to each other, but the truth was that if Brand wanted to continue seeing Lorraine or any other woman he pleased, there was nothing she could do to stop it. He had trapped her and he knew it, because if she tried to leave him again, he would prosecute Dale.

Rockport was a small coastal town with a shrimping, boat-building, and tourist economy. Melody had always liked it for its fishbowl harbor and its live oak trees that were knotted and bent into tortuous, surrealistic shapes from hundreds of years of gulf winds and hurricanes. Brand's grandparents lived in a waterfront condominium, where they had moved after the elder Mr. Travers gave up ranching in favor of retirement.

Melody had spoken no less than the truth when she told Brand she loved them. They had been good to the shy, inexperienced young bride she had been, and there would always be a soft spot in her heart for them, but as they reached the outskirts of town, she tensed with dread that this time they would not be so welcoming. And if they were not, it would be bound to upset Brand, for he was very close to them. His own mother had died when Tammy was only four years old and his father had died shortly after they had been married, leaving them and his grandparents to all do their best to raise the child.

She need not have worried about Gram and Gramps, she thought ruefully half an hour later, but Tammy was something else. Odd how she had gotten her concerns exactly opposite. Despite old Juanita's revelation, it had not seriously occurred to Melody that Tammy would not be glad to see her, and so it was with a sense of shock that she realized that the girl was holding her off with actual dislike.

They were all having coffee on the balcony overlooking the boat channel. Gramps' motorboat, which he used

51

almost daily for the fishing trips he enjoyed, was tied below at the pier. In the distance lay a placid, blue-glass Aransas Bay.

Melody was pleased to note that the passage of time seemed hardly to have touched Brand's grandparents since she had last seen them. Gramps's hair was perhaps a little grayer and Gram was maybe a few pounds stouter, but that was about all. Both appeared to be just as spry and energetic as ever, despite Brand's statement to the contrary, though Melody knew that appearances could be, and often were, deceptive.

As Gram passed around slices of a raisin cake she had baked, Gramps, who sat beside Melody, asked, "Do you still like to water-ski?"

She smiled at him and gave a tiny shrug. "I do, but I just never get the chance to anymore."

"Then we'll take you for a go-round sometime soon," he promised. "Tammy is getting to be quite an expert at it herself." They both glanced across at the girl, but she resolutely turned her head to look away from them, unwilling to be drawn into the conversation. Gramps continued after a moment with a chuckle, "If I remember correctly, that's how you and Brand met, wasn't it?"

"That's right, Gramps." It was Brand who answered the question. "There was a large group of us picnicking and water-skiing one Sunday afternoon and Melody came with one of my friends' younger brother."

"Poor young man," Gram said with a shake of her head and a twinkle in her sea-blue eyes. "He went home alone that day because you," she nodded toward Brand, "were such a dreadful buccanneer that you kidnapped Melody and carried her off yourself."

Melody laughed self-consciously and hated herself for blushing. She happened to catch Brand watching her and there was a lighthearted teasing expression in his dark eyes that stopped her heart. If she didn't know better . . .

But, she caught herself up sharply, she did know better.

That tender look of love was being put on for the others' benefit, not hers.

"I hope he didn't have to kidnap you this time, my dear, in order to bring you back again," Gramps said after the laughter died down.

Now there was a mocking glint in the dark eyes that she understood perfectly. She wondered what Brand would do if she told Gramps the truth . . . that instead of kidnapping her this time, he had blackmailed her.

Before Melody could think of a response, Gram said fondly, "Well, I for one don't care how it happened. I'm just glad it did. It's wonderful to have you back with us again, Melody, and it's so romantic."

"Yuk!" Tammy said with a thick coating of disgust overlaying the outburst. "I think it's all stupid!" She was perching on the wooden balcony railing, her straight black hair whipping in wild tangles away from her sullen face.

"Tammy!" Gram spoke sharply. "I think you owe Melody and Brand an apology."

"Why?" Tammy straightened and got to her feet. At fifteen, she was slightly on the plump side, although her body had enough curves in the right places that it could have been lovely if she only lost a few pounds and replaced the scowl on her face with a smile. She wore faded jean shorts and a wrinkled red-and-white T-shirt and her feet were bare. Now she padded across the balcony to stand facing the others. "I think their getting married again was a dumb thing to do, so why shouldn't I say so? Nobody ever bothers to find out how *I* feel about anything," she said accusingly. "Brand and I were doing just fine without anyone else around. We don't need Melody!"

This time Brand's steel voice chastised his sister. "You will apologize to Melody at once, Tam. At once!" The last words struck her with the sting of a whip.

Melody winced, knowing and hating the fact that she was the cause of Brand's anger with his sister, and she sat in frozen silence as Tammy glared at Brand for a long, strained moment before she finally lowered her head and mumbled, "Sorry."

"Th-that's okay, Tammy," Melody said huskily. "I understand."

"No!" Tammy exclaimed shrilly as she jerked her head up. "You *don't* understand. Nobody does."

"That's enough, Tammy," Brand said with crisp authority. "Whether you believe we understand or not, I expect you to behave with civility and respect toward Melody. Besides, now that she's with us, it'll mean I won't have to send you away to boarding school again. Doesn't that please you?"

"Big deal!" Tammy grumbled sarcastically as she moved toward the door. "I'm going inside. I've still got to finish packing."

Melody started to rise to follow her, but Brand waved her back into her chair and, silently, they all waited until the girl was out of hearing.

Gram sighed. "I'm sure I just don't understand young people anymore. Tammy used to be the sweetest child."

Melody appealed to Brand. "Maybe I ought to go in and speak with her," she began.

Brand cut her off with a curt shake of his head. "No. She was rude to you and she can just sulk all alone. Relax and visit with Gram. You'll have enough chances to deal with Tammy when we get home."

A little later, Melody went inside with Gram to help her prepare the midday meal, while Brand kept his grandfather company outside. Tammy's bedroom door remained firmly closed.

"I hate to say this, Melody," the older lady told her as she began slicing some cucumbers, "but I'm afraid you're going to have your hands full with Tammy. Brand can usually handle her quite well because he simply won't stand for her scenes, but for any of the rest of us it's not so easy."

"So I noticed," Melody agreed drily as she tied an

apron around her waist. "What's happened to her, Gram?"

Gram gave an expressive shrug. "I don't really know. She's been growing worse for a long time now. It seems like every time she comes back from one of those schools, she's worse than the time before. And yet she's not a bad child." She sighed. "She's not on drugs and she doesn't do any of the awful things like some teenagers these days. It's just that she makes everyone miserable by her attitude . . . the way she was today."

Melody nodded thoughtfully as she picked up a stack of plates to carry to the table. "Tammy and I used to be quite close," she said musingly. "Maybe I can find a way to reach her again."

"I sincerely hope so," Gram said, "but don't be disappointed if you fail like the rest of us, honey. Now," she ordered cheerfully, changing the subject, "tell me all about you and Brand and how you suddenly got back together again. I'm so pleased for you. I always knew that Brand was an unhappy and incomplete man without you, despite burying himself in his work the way he did."

"Unhappy?" Melody asked blankly as she went very still.

Gram nodded firmly. "Of course he was. No matter what the trouble was between you, he was completely lost without you. It took you a long time to decide to come back," she chided gently.

"Yes," Melody answered vaguely. "Well, it took a long time before he wanted me to come back, Gram."

"Pride," Gram said with instant perception. "I'd be willing to bet more marriages have been broken up over pride than over anything else, and that's pretty cold comfort alone in bed at night."

Melody's face burned. Brand's grandmother, noticing it, chuckled and turned back to the sink, where she began vigorously scraping a carrot. "I don't mean to embarrass you, child. I'm just pointing out how futile some arguments can be, and how devastating the effects. But you

55

two are back together now, you're both older and wiser, and I'm sure neither of you will ever allow anything silly to tear you apart again."

"You . . . you have a lot of faith in us, Gram," Melody said in a quivering voice. "I . . . I hope we can justify it."

Gram's gaze was speculative and she turned to look at her again. "It's your faith in yourselves that counts, honey. If you love each other enough to look beyond fault-finding and pride, you'll make it."

And that, thought Melody as she set the table, was the trouble. Now there *was* no love involved, but Gram did not know that. Her mind flitted briefly to Rob, and she wondered whether their marriage would have worked if it had occurred. Rob was a rather easygoing man, not volatile and dynamic as was Brand, and that was what had attracted her to him. He did not demand all of one the way Brand did, and with him she could relax and not feel pressured in any way. And yet, in her heart, she knew that what she had felt for Rob had been comfortable familiarity rather than love. And if love, which she and Brand had had the first time, could not hold them together, how could her marriage to Rob have possibly endured?

Now she was glad they had not married. It would not have been fair to Rob, she realized for the first time. She would have cheated him out of the most important possession in the world. For herself, though, it was different. She did not love Brand now . . . he had killed it himself. But neither had she loved Rob, so she supposed it really did not matter that she was married to Brand again. She suspected she was incapable of ever experiencing that emotion again, so in that case it made no difference that she was involved in a loveless match, as long as the man in question did not love her either. Brand had said that this time they were married for good. Perhaps, she thought bitterly, in the end hate was more binding than love.

The drive back home that afternoon was accomplished in near silence. Brand seemed preoccupied with his own thoughts and kept his attention almost entirely on the highway; Melody made a few abortive attempts to engage in conversation with Tammy, but the girl answered her only in curt monosyllables.

Melody was relieved when they arrived home at last and she could be free to escape from the heavy, strained atmosphere in the car. She went straight upstairs to the bedroom and changed into her bathing suit while Brand went into his study and Tammy went to her room.

A few minutes later, Melody plunged into the cool waters of the pool and energetically swam a few laps to release some of the tension in her body. It was exactly what she needed, and gradually she felt more herself, calm, and even a little cheerful, even though her solitude was shattered a short time later when both Brand and Tammy came out.

Tammy still wore her shorts and shirt, and she flopped down ungracefully in one of the pool-side lounge chairs, but Brand had changed into blue swim trunks.

Melody looked up at him in surprise. "I assumed you'd be going off to the office for a while."

He raised quizzical eyebrows. "On Saturday afternoon?"

"I'd forgotten what day it is," she admitted as he dropped his towel on an empty chair and came toward the pool. She glanced over at Tammy, who was watching her with open hostility. "Why don't you get into your bathing suit and join us?"

Tammy shook her head. "I'm not in the mood. The only reason I'm here is because my big brother insisted on my company."

Melody shrugged her wet shoulders. "Suit yourself," she said as she turned to watch Brand dive into the water.

His head emerged a moment later only a yard away from her, then he turned and, with long, sure strokes, swam the length of the pool.

When Juanita brought out cold drinks for them a little

later, Melody climbed out of the pool and dried herself, feeling quite naked in her bikini as Brand joined her and put his arm possessively around her waist.

"Sure you don't want a mixed drink yourself?" he asked as he picked up his glass from the table.

She shook her head. "No, thanks," she answered as she reached for a glass of lemonade. "You know it would only give me a headache." Deftly, she removed herself from his arm and went over to drop down into a chair beside Tammy.

"How come you wouldn't come in?" she asked now, determined to break through Tammy's sullen defenses. "You used to adore swimming."

Tammy shrugged. "What would be the fun of it with only you two?"

Brand came and sat on the edge of Melody's chair, and this time his hand went around her shoulders. Melody tensed as every nerve in her body was quiveringly aware of his touch, but she tried to ignore the sensation and concentrate instead on Tammy.

"Then why don't you invite some of your friends over to swim with you?" she suggested mildly. "You could have them over tomorrow afternoon."

"Oh, sure," Tammy said sarcastically, "I could do that, all right, *if* I happened to have any friends, which I don't." She stared gloweringly down at the drink in her hand.

Melody frowned, not understanding. "But, Tammy, you used to have masses of friends around here."

The girl shrugged once more, still keeping her eyes averted from the others. "Not anymore, I don't," she denied in a stony voice. "I've been away to school so long I don't have any friends left here."

"Or anywhere else," Brand stated unequivocally. "But it's your own fault, Tam. In order to have friends, you have to first *be* a friend to others, and you certainly have to behave in a friendly way. Nobody enjoys being around someone who is always in a rotten mood."

Tammy jumped to her feet and her face was red with

58

anger. "In that case," she said through quivering lips, "I'll remove myself from your presence so my rotten mood won't rub off on you." Whirling, she went swiftly around the house.

Brand made a sound filled with exasperation. "She's worse since she came home from school this time than ever." He looked down at Melody's upturned face and his hand tightened on her shoulder. "Do you think you can straighten her out? Can you reach her?"

Melody shook her head slowly. "I don't know," she admitted honestly. "Tammy seems to resent me so much now. She's completely unapproachable—not at all like the girl I remember."

Brand's black eyes turned into two hard marbles. "Nevertheless," he said in a grim voice, "I expect you to try. After all, it's the least you can do after abandoning us like you did five years ago and creating such hell for everyone."

Melody jerked away from his touch as though she had been struck by a rattler. She was shocked at the barely suppressed violence in his manner. He was coldly furious with her.

Anger she had buried deeply for years surged to the surface of her own emotions. "You act just as though you were the innocent, injured party instead of me!" she gasped.

His eyes narrowed. "What are you talking about?" he demanded.

"Nothing!" Her voice was shaking as she struggled to her feet. "The past is over and frankly," she added with unmistakable scorn, "I just don't care anymore!"

His arm shot out and his hand clamped over her wrist in a viselike grasp. "You've hinted at something before," he said harshly, "and I want to know what you mean."

"Brand," she objected, "you're hurting me!" She tried to pull her arm free from his strong grip.

"I'll do more than this if you don't tell me," he rasped out. "I'm tired of your innuendos."

"And I'm tired of your outraged innocent act," she retorted cuttingly. "My God, what a fool you take me for . . . *took* me for!"

"Mr. Travers!" Opal's voice cut through the thick haze of their anger as they stood glaring at each other. "Miss White is on the telephone and she wants to speak to you."

Brand dropped her arm, and with one last angry glance he turned and left her standing there while he went inside to take Lorraine's call.

Chapter Five

Melody stood on the fishing pier, breathing in the tangy salt air and the fishy smell that piers always seemed to have. The wind whipped her copper-toned hair away from her hot face and neck, cooling her skin. She was wearing a deep blue jogging shorts set and already, just from the few days she had been there, her arms and legs had turned a golden, toasty hue. She knew from experience that before summer was out she would be very tanned indeed, for not being a true redhead, but having more brown pigments in her hair, she always darkened instead of burning.

She leaned against the railing and gazed idly across the bay toward the skyline of the city. The tall buildings of downtown and uptown on the bluff merged as they thrust upward, creating a jagged, uneven backdrop against the brilliant blue of the sky. Further away, filmed with haze, was the harbor bridge.

She had been on the pier for almost two hours, ostensibly fishing, but it had been a halfhearted attempt at best. Actually, she had hoped the lapping song of the waves and the constant breeze would soothe her nerves as well as provide a brief means of escaping the house and Tammy.

Melody sighed and stared morosely down at the waves thrusting eternally against the shore. It had been several days since Tammy had come home and they had been miserable days. The girl was rude, arrogant, and consistently sullen, and nothing anybody tried seemed to help. The atmosphere whenever she was in a room was always fraught with tension and conflict. Melody wanted to help her, but Tammy resented her so much the very idea was ludicrous. Brand had made a terrible mistake in thinking she could do so.

Things had not been any better with Brand either, lately, she thought now, as she shifted her position against the rails. True, she had seen little of him the past few days since he had been working long hours at the office, but whenever he was at home his humor had seemed no better than his sister's. Right now Melody felt imprisoned within a thick vapor of hostility and it could not help but adversely affect her own emotions.

She was depressed and her energy level was down. She knew she should get away from this place for a few hours. Brand had purchased a new, pale green Buick for her use, but she had scarcely used it. There was no place in particular that she cared to go. What she really needed was some congenial company, something she had lacked since the visit with Brand's grandparents, but that brought up another problem. She shied away from contacting any of her old friends from the past. She was unsure how she would be received, because they had been Brand's friends as well, and for now it simply seemed easier to let things slide. Still, she was bored with her own company and even Dale had not come around to visit the past few days. She felt entirely cut off from the normal world.

Melody became aware that she was developing the beginnings of a slight headache from standing so long in the glaring sun without a hat for protection, so she gathered her fishing gear and slowly made her way up the steps that led to the top of the bluff, reluctant, still, to return to the house.

"No fish?" a polite voice enquired as she reached the lawn.

Smiling, she shook her head. "Hardly even a nibble,

Barney," she told the gardener, who was weeding a flower bed.

Barney got to his feet and came across to her. "I'll put your gear away," he offered, and as she handed it to him he added, "Fishing off the pier's not what it used to be. Best thing is to get Mr. Travers to take you out in the boat and fish near one of the oil platforms."

Melody nodded. "You're right, of course." She resumed her way across the lawn, and as she reached the patio she found Tammy there, devouring a bowl of chocolate ice cream. This time she had to force a smile to her lips. "My, it's sure hot," she stated casually. "I can't decide whether I want a swim or a shower. If I swim, will you join me?"

Tammy shook her head. "I'm not in the mood. Besides, " she added almost unwillingly, "I can't fit into my old bathing suit anymore."

"Is that all that's holding you back?" Melody asked in amazement. "If you'd like, we can go shopping for one this afternoon."

Tammy grimaced. "So I can look like a Sherman tank beside you?" she said. "No, thanks."

Melody watched her thoughtfully for a moment, then she ventured, "If your weight is bothering you, you could always go on a diet. I could help you plan one."

"I'm quite happy with myself as I am," Tammy said curtly, "and I sure don't need your help . . . for anything!"

"Have it your own way," Melody said as she started to move toward the door. "But I have to say this, Tam. You'd be a very beautiful girl if you would just drop some of those pounds along with your sour disposition. However"—she shrugged her shoulders with a careless motion—"it's your life."

"Just get off my back," Tammy snapped. "I don't *need* your sermons, okay?"

Melody went into the house and up the stairs, furious with herself for having even attempted to reason with

Tammy. It had been a waste of breath and had only created one more ugly little scene.

At dinner that evening, there was another, even uglier scene, and unwittingly, Melody set it off herself.

There were only the three of them, and though Tammy was silent, intent only on her food, Brand and Melody were making meaningless conversation just to keep up the appearance of happily marrieds.

"Sometime soon I'd like to drive out to Padre Island," Melody said.

"You'll be amazed at how much it has built up the past few years," Brand told her. "More houses, condominiums, a golf course. The county park, though, is about like it always was."

"I suppose Bob Hall Pier is still there?"

Brand nodded. "Oh, sure, and always packed with fishermen, as usual. I haven't driven down as far as Malaquite Beach in quite a while," he added, referring to the Padre Island National Seashore, "but I suppose it's still the same. If you want to go, why don't you and Tammy pack a lunch and go out and spend a day sometime soon?"

Melody turned to Tammy. "How about it?" she asked. "Would you like spending a day on the island?"

"Not with you!" Tammy snapped. Her dark eyes flashed. "I hate you and I don't want anything to do with you! Can't you understand that?" She shoved back her chair, knocking it over as she got to her feet.

Melody's face went white and her body was paralyzed as the words assaulted her.

Brand's own chair was thrust backward and he stood towering over the table with a menacing expression on his face. Swiftly, he rounded the table, roughly grabbed Tammy's shoulders and began to shake her. "I will not tolerate this sort of thing any longer, Tammy," he told her in a voice that chilled Melody. "You have behaved horribly ever since you got home, but now you have gone too far. Melody is my wife and as such she will receive not only obedience from you, but respect and courtesy as well. You will apologize to her now, and in the future you will behave agreeably to her."

He turned her forcibly so that she was facing Melody and the girl's face was red with a mixture of anger and humiliation. She glared across the table with such hatred and resentment that Melody flinched. What on earth had she done to cause Tammy to hate her so, she wondered desperately.

There was a long, tense period when no one spoke and then Brand's commanding voice rang out. "Tammy!"

Tammy ducked her head and mumbled inaudibly, "Sorry."

"I didn't hear you," Brand told her in a voice of steel.

"I did." Melody spoke up sharply. "Leave her alone, Brand. I heard her. Please, let . . . let's all forget about this and . . . and just finish dinner," she pleaded.

Brand's face was stormy as he watched his sister. "Tammy has already finished with her dinner."

Tammy whirled to face him. "I have not!" she said hotly. "I only just started!"

"That's too bad, isn't it?" Brand told her. "But tonight you have finished. I will not tolerate rude behavior at my table."

"Brand, please," Melody begged. "She apologized. Can't we just drop it? There's no need to send her away."

Now the angry dark eyes were trained on her. "You will not interfere with my discipline," he told her in a grating voice. Then he glanced at Tammy again. "You may go," he told her coldly.

Tammy gave them both a furious look before she flounced out of the room. There was a long, pregnant silence and then Brand picked up Tammy's chair and set it upright before resuming his seat.

Melody's own appetite had deserted her, though Brand ate calmly as though nothing had happened.

She licked her lips. "Brand," she began hesitantly, "Tammy hates me. You even heard her say so."

He raised his eyes to meet hers briefly. "And?"

"And . . . well, she was the reason you said you wanted to marry me again . . . so that I could help you raise her. But it isn't working, and as long as she resents me like this, it isn't likely to ever work, so . . . so why don't you just let me go?"

His dark brows lowered ominously over his eyes. "Back to Dallas?" he asked.

She nodded.

"Back to that man you were engaged to?" His voice washed over her with the coldness of ice water.

Now she shook her head. "N-no. Only away from here. You don't love me, so you can't want me here for yourself, and surely you can see I'm the wrong person to deal with Tammy. It would be better all the way around if I just went away again."

"No," he said tautly. "You're staying here and that's final."

She had to try again. "But Tammy . . ." she began.

"Let's get this straight," he told her. "Right now I'm not particularly concerned with what either you or Tammy want. You'll both do as I say. Ah, yes, Juanita," he said in a completely normal voice as he looked up to see the cook enter the room, "we would like some coffee, thank you."

It stormed during the night. Melody awoke suddenly as a crash of thunder reverberated throughout the house. The rain came heavily, beating with ferocious violence against the windowpanes.

She shifted her position in the bed and as she did so Brand turned too, and his arm slid across her bare legs. A flash of lightning illuminated the room and she could see his face, calm and pleasant as though he were enjoying his dream.

She wished she could understand him, but he was vastly changed from the man she had once loved. Most of the time he was thoroughly rude and callous toward her, except when they they were in the company of others.

Then would come an abrupt change and he would treat her lovingly as she supposed a man might if he had just remarried his ex-wife because he *was* in love with her. Only a few times had she so much as caught even a glimpse of the old Brand, with his natural and easy smile and genuine openness. It was as though he were closely guarding himself against her, determined not to allow her to find the man he really was.

It suddenly occurred to her that she was doing the same thing. She was no more the girl he had first married than he was the same man. Too much had happened, too many bitter years had come between for it to be so. She guarded her own feelings just as diligently from his piercing eyes, sternly keeping under lock and key any remembered tenderness they had once shared. But just now, while he was vulnerable in his sleep, she was shocked to discover a tiny flare of old emotions she had long thought dead, and she knotted her fists tightly to stem a sudden overpowering desire to reach out her hand and touch his face or to bury her own head in the curve of his neck, where she had slept so many, many nights in the past.

It was insane, and Melody turned over again so that she was facing away from her huband. What, she asked herself wildly, had come over her? For a long time she stared out the window at the rain and the flashes of lightning, but by the time she finally fell asleep again, she still did not have the answer.

It rained off and on throughout the following day and Melody felt the confinement even more keenly, for today there was no walking down to the pier or swimming in the pool. She moved through the house like an aimless ghost. There was nothing for her to do. Between them, Juanita and Opal had the house well in hand, and Tammy was shut away in her bedroom. Melody had been too used to an active life to appreciate enforced idleness, and finally, as a desperate measure, she took the car and went shopping.

She bought a pretty white sundress for Tammy and a new tube of lipstick for herself, and though she was not gone over two hours, the outing gave her a new sense of release.

When she walked into the house with her package, Tammy met her in the hall. "Where've you been?" she demanded belligerently.

Melody surveyed her coolly as she shrugged off her raincoat. "Shopping," she answered briefly.

"You missed lunch."

"I ate at a restaurant."

Tammy gave her a disgruntled look. "You might have invited me along. It's boring stuck in this house."

Melody's eyebrows lifted. "I didn't know you'd be interested. I've invited you before and you refused," she reminded mildly. Now she held out the large package in her hand. "Here, I bought you a new dress. Why don't you try it on and see if you like it?"

Tammy looked at her suspiciously, but she took the package and opened it. She stared for a long time at the dress before saying in a flat voice, "You wasted your money. I don't have anywhere to go to wear it."

Melody shrugged her shoulders. "Well, it's yours if it fits and you want it. Perhaps an occasion will arise so that you can wear it sometime. Excuse me, but I'm tired and I'm going up to my room." Without another word, she walked away, and once she was out of sight, a tiny, grim smile played across her lips. Tammy had been unhappy because she had not been invited along on the shopping trip, and she had not outright refused the dress! Maybe there was hope yet!

The following morning was bright with light and freshly washed from the rain of the previous day. A shaft of sunlight dancing across her face awoke Melody. She stretched lazily, listening to the mingled sounds of a sparrow singing outside the window and the shower running in the bathroom.

A few minutes later Brand came into the room, wrapped as usual in a thick terrycloth towel. He was freshly shaved and his wet hair glistened. He saw that she was awake and smiled. "Good morning," he said cheerfully.

"Good morning." She could not help but return the smile. The way his smile softened the firmness of his lips and made crinkle lines at the corners of his eyes had always compelled her response. She had not seen this real, unaffected smile of his for a long, long time.

"It's a beautiful day," he commented idly as he walked over to the closet.

"Yes, it is," she agreed, as her gaze took in the breadth of his shoulders and the sinewy muscles that rippled beneath his skin.

"Are you hungry?" he asked, turning slightly to glance over his shoulder at her.

"Now that you mention it, yes," she laughed as her stomach grumbled.

Brand smiled again. "Why don't you get dressed and have breakfast with me? I'll ask Juanita to serve it on the patio."

"That's a lovely idea," she answered as she sat upright in the bed and stretched her arms out. "All right. Give me fifteen minutes."

"Ten," Brand ordered as she threw back the covers and got to her feet. "I'm starving, and," he added with a definitely teasing glint to his eyes, "you look so delectable in that nighty I just might be tempted to assuage other appetites if you don't hurry!"

Melody's face pinkened and a nervous laugh caught in her throat. Brand was looking at her as though, as though . . . she could not put it into words. She only knew that today he was different—warmer and more friendly—and, oddly, it made her feel slightly threatened, as though she were confronted with some subtle danger that she could not quite identify.

She ·felt better equipped to deal with him twenty minutes later, as, dressed in a pair of beige slacks and an eggshell-white blouse, she sat across the patio table from him.

Juanita brought them sausage and pancakes and they talked idly and companionably as they ate. Melody was amazed that it was so because it was the very first time they had been together without any undercurrents of tension between them.

There were already a few fishing boats far out in the bay and a couple of sailboats gliding like graceful butterflies across the shimmering, gold-gilded water. Seeing her watching the boats, Brand said, "Sometime soon we'll take out the *Tammy II* if you like."

Melody's eyes sparkled and a smile stretched her soft lips. "I'd love it," she admitted.

They had finished their breakfast and now Brand pushed back his chair and stood up. He surprised her by walking around to her side of the table. "It's been nice, Melody," he said in a low, resonant voice, "but much as I'd like to stay here with you, it's time I got to work."

"Of . . . course," she stammered. His nearness was affecting her senses. She was throbbingly aware of everything about him—his towering height, the darkness of his hair and eyes, the sun-browned color of his skin, the way his neat navy-blue suit fitted him so perfectly, even the masculine smell of him.

His hand came out and touched a lock of her hair and she was mesmerized by the action. Then he bent and kissed her lips, a gentle, incredibly tender kiss that took her breath away.

He was smiling as he straightened up again. "You're very beautiful this morning," he told her with a slight huskiness breaking his voice. Then, with a lighthearted raise of his hand, he added casually, "See you tonight." And he was gone.

Determinedly, Melody thrust her confusing thoughts of Brand into the recesses of her mind. It was too lovely a day to spend analyzing either his behavior or her own responses. The truth was she was half afraid of the answers. It was well, she told herself, to remember the past, the reason why she was here.

She busied herself working with the numerous hanging plants that gave such luxurious color to the patio. Far from being offended that his own area was being invaded, Barney cheerfully helped her carry the gardening supplies from the storage building and offered her a running stream of advice, before returning to his flower beds.

She was on her knees, thrusting cuttings of an ivy into potting soil, when Opal came to tell her she was wanted on the telephone. Melody got to her feet at once, brushing off her slacks and flexing cramped muscles. It was probably Dale, she decided as she went into the house. He hadn't called in several days.

"Melody?" a lilting voice enquired after she picked up the receiver in Brand's study. "This is Nicole. Nicole Simon."

"Well, hello!" Melody exclaimed with pleasure. "How are you, Nicole?"

"Angry," came the prompt reply. "I only just found out about you and Brand being back together. Why haven't you called me? Don't you want to see your old friends anymore?"

"Of course I do," Melody answered quickly. "It was just that I've been quite busy," she fibbed, and then with a sudden gush of words, she admitted the truth. "I . . . actually, I guess I wasn't sure if you'd want to see me."

"Idiot," Nicole said fondly. "Of course I do. We always considered you our friend as much as Brand is, and I was hurt when you never wrote or called me all those years."

"I'm sorry," Melody mumbled. "I wanted to, but . . ." She shrugged, forgetting Nicole could not see the gesture. "I supposed a clean break with the past was best."

"Hmm. Well, it doesn't matter," Nicole went on, "since you're back now and you and Brand are together again. Listen, the reason I'm calling is that Carl and I want to

70

invite you, Brand, and Tammy to come for a barbecue tomorrow evening. How about it . . . are you free?"

"I'd love it," Melody said warmly. "That is, if Brand doesn't have anything planned. I'll need to check with him first, of course, and call you back."

"Fine," her old friend said. "I hope you can make it. We'll have a great time catching up on the years. I'm dying to show off our two little monsters to you, too."

"Two?" Melody asked with interest. "How old are they?"

"Four and two and a half. Both boys and do they ever keep me running!"

Melody laughed. "I'm sure they do and I can't wait to see them. I'll call you back, Nicole, just as soon as I check with Brand."

She smiled to herself as she dialed Brand's office. Nicole and Carl Simon had been their closest friends when she and Brand had been married before. The two couples had often been together, taking short trips to Mexico or deep-sea fishing besides sharing a dinner at least once a week. Of course then Nicole and Simon had been childless, too, and as free to come and go as she and Brand. She felt a tiny twinge of envy now. Her own life the last five years had been fruitless and barren while Nicole's had been busy, full of purpose and love.

Melody gave Brand's name to the receptionist who answered the telephone, but a moment later, instead of Brand's strong voice, Lorraine's came on the line.

"Mr. Travers' office," she said with professional crispness. "May I help you?"

"Yes. I'd like to speak to Brand, please. This is his wife calling."

"Sorry," Lorraine said with an abrupt change in her manner. "He's in conference and he wouldn't thank me to disturb him for domestic trivia."

Melody sucked in a sharp breath. The woman was unbelievable! With a coldness in her own voice matching that of the secretary's, she said, "I wouldn't wish to disturb him while he's in conference, either. Have him call me at home as soon as he is free."

"I don't take orders from anyone except Brand," Lorraine hissed. "Certainly not from you!"

Now Melody's voice was sugar sweet. "Lorraine, it's part of a secretary's duty to pass messages on to her boss. *Especially* when the message is from his wife. I doubt if Brand will be too pleased when he arrives home tonight to discover that he wasn't told I had called."

"You think you hold all the cards, don't you?" Lorraine rasped out furiously. "But you'll lose in the end and he'll be mine . . . all mine! You're the biggest mistake that ever happened to Brand and it's only a matter of time until he sees it! You have nothing whatsoever to offer him!" There was a loud bang and Melody realized Lorraine had hung up.

She was more shaken by the incident than she would have believed. She sank into Brand's leather desk chair and stared blankly at the book-lined walls. What had begun as a beautiful day was now gray and dismal. Lorraine's poisonous venom seemed to have been injected into her bloodstream and her stomach churned with nausea.

Yes, the day was definitely spoiled and the earlier warmth, even tenderness between herself and Brand was rendered meaningless. She had been most forcefully reminded that she had no real place in Brand's life and that nothing should be taken at face value.

When Brand's call came a half hour later, Melody had gained a hard grip on herself and was totally indifferent to the warmth in his voice. "Hi, sorry I was tied up when you called, but it was a long-winded client. Did you call about something in particular or because you missed me?" The last was said in a teasing vein.

Melody's fingernails dug into her palm as the rest of her body went rigid. "I called," she said in a tone devoid of all emotion, "to tell you Nicole and Carl invited us to a barbecue tomorrow night."

"That's great," he said with enthusiasm. "Tell Nicole yes. You'll enjoy seeing them again, I know."

"Of course," she answered politely. "Then I won't keep you any longer. I . . ."

"Melody," Brand said sharply. "What's the matter?"

"I don't know what you mean," she said through stiff lips.

"I mean something's wrong. You've changed since this morning."

Damn him! she thought angrily. He had always been able to read her moods too clearly for comfort. But she had no intention of enlightening him. "There's nothing wrong that hasn't been wrong all along," she told him. "You've turned me into your prisoner. Do you expect me to be happy about that?"

She heard him give a muttered oath. "You seemed to be happy enough this morning," he said with nasty sarcasm. "What happened? Did you let yourself go and forget the circumstances for a while?"

"Exactly," she answered through gritted teeth.

An instant later the line went dead. For the second time that day a person had hung up on her.

Chapter Six

She had never felt less in the mood for socializing in her life, Melody decided. Looking coolly remote in an aqua sundress and with her hair swept up into a sophisticated knot on her head, she sat in tense silence as Brand, in casual tan slacks and a brown pullover knit shirt, drove them to the Simons'. It had been a bad day and all three of them were at odds. Tammy, in the back seat, gazed stonily out the window; Brand drove with a taut grimness to his face.

Brand had come home from the office last night in a bad humor, brought on because of their earlier telephone conversation. This morning there had been no repeat of the thawing between them yesterday. Brand had risen in silence, while Melody deliberately pretended to still be asleep.

Today had brought another scene with Tammy. She had flatly refused to go along to the Simons' tonight and Melody had not been able to sway her. And then Brand had come home and curtly ordered her to go with them, which had precipitated another scene. Finally, the girl had given in, albeit with ill grace, but when she had come downstairs to join them, she had been wearing jeans and a stained T-shirt, which had brought on yet another explosion of wrath from Brand. Now Tammy was wearing the white sundress that Melody had bought for her, but her angry expression completely detracted attention from the attractiveness of the dress.

Melody gave an inward sigh and reached up a hand to rub her tense neck. She had a throbbing headache from all the strife and though she had taken a couple of aspirins an hour ago, the pain had not diminished in the least. Far from looking happily toward a pleasant evening with old friends, she yearned only for bed and quiet solitude.

The Simons lived in a sprawling ranch-style house and on both sides of the the front walk grew yuccas, century plants, and a large variety of cactus.

Carl answered the door, attired in jeans, a Western shirt with the sleeves rolled up above his elbows, and a large white apron that boasted the words, "World's Greatest Chef."

"Hello, hello," he greeted heartily. "Come on in. Nicole will be out in a minute. She's giving the boys their baths." He shook Brand's hand, told Tammy she had turned into a lovely young lady since the last time he had seen her, which caused her to scowl, and then he enveloped Melody in a bear hug. An instant later, holding her at arm's length, he said critically, "A bit skinnier than you used to be, but even so you're more beautiful than ever!"

"Thanks, Carl." Melody smiled. "And you look less like a dignified obstetrician ought to than any doctor I ever saw! If your patients could see you in that apron, they would instantly lose all confidence in you!"

Carl grinned. "What they don't know won't hurt them," he said with a casual shrug. "Besides, it's true. If I ever get tired of delivering babies I can always open up a barbecue stand. Come on out to the patio," he invited them. "I've got the mesquite burning down and it won't be long until I can throw on the steaks."

On the patio they found a teenaged boy playing with a cocker spaniel. He stood up at once as they all trooped out.

"This is my nephew, Jim Simon, who has come from Lubbock to spend the summer with us," Carl said by way of introduction. "Jim, this is Brand and Melody Travers and Brand's sister, Tammy."

He was a tall, lanky, nice-looking boy of about sixteen, Melody observed as he came forward to shake hands. His hair, which grew just below his ears, was a silvery blond and his blue eyes had a clear, direct gaze.

He spoke politely to both Brand and her, but his face turned a dull red as he spoke to Tammy. Tammy's own color heightened also.

Compassionately, Melody drew attention away from them, reflecting to herself that teenagers could be exuberantly outgoing or shy and extremely sensitive. "Carl," she said, "your patio is lovely. I like that brick border fence. You didn't have it before."

"No, we built it last year. You . . ."

Carl got no further because Nicole, a small, vivacious woman with dark hair and a bright smile, joined them. "Melody!" Nicole flung her arms around Melody. "I'm *so* pleased to see you again. Come inside at once and meet the boys. They're in their pajamas ready for bed, but I didn't want to let them go to sleep until after you got here.

Carl," she added as an afterthought as she gripped Melody's arm and began to tug her away, "haven't you offered your guests a drink yet? Where are your manners, honey?"

Her husband laughed good-naturedly at her and then the two women went inside.

The children were darlings and Melody fell in love with them at once. Tommy, at four, was a chatterer and he had his mother's dark good looks; Jason, not yet three, was more silent, but already a heart-breaker with long golden lashes that were devastatingly flirtatious, combined as they were with his beguiling smile and his father's blond hair.

"You must be so proud of them, Nicole," Melody said warmly after they had both tucked the boys into their beds with goodnight kisses.

Nicole's eyes sparkled. "You're so right, Melody—especially when they're sweet and clean and ready for bed. However, when they're cranky and dirty from playing in a mud puddle . . ." They both laughed at that, and then Nicole added, "Now that you and Brand are back together, it's high time you got started on your own family, don't you think?"

Melody paled at the thought, but she forced a smile to her lips as she realized her friend was watching her closely.

"Don't rush me," she said lightly. "After all, I haven't been back very long yet."

Nicole grinned. "Still on your second honeymoon, are you?" she asked slyly.

"S-something like that," Melody agreed warily. Then she hurried to change the subject. "Carl says his nephew is here for the summer?"

Nicole nodded. "Yes. His father is going to be away on a number of business trips the next few months so his mother is going to spend the summer with her relatives in Iowa. Jim wanted to come here instead. He's always been our favorite out of all the family so I'm sure it will work out all right. My main concern is for him to meet some friends his own age. I do hope Tammy and he hit it off all right."

Both teenagers seemed to be scrupulously avoiding each other, she noticed at once. Tammy was staring at a rosebush with a distant expression on her face. Jim had returned to the cocker spaniel and was throwing a stick and urging the dog to fetch it.

Brand came forward, a drink in his hand, and, to Melody's surprise, draped a casual arm across her shoulder. "Well, what did you think of the little livewires, darling?" he asked.

Her shoulders tensed. Darling! It was the first time Brand had called her that in years, and the realization that he did it now only for effect infuriated her. She squirmed beneath his arm, but if she hoped it would cause him to remove it, she was mistaken. His hand tightened on her shoulder, his fingers pressing into flesh, and there was a warning light in his eyes as they met hers.

"We're two ahead of you, Brand," Carl chuckled before Melody could answer. "You'd better get busy and catch up."

Melody's face scalded. What was it with Nicole and Carl that they felt the need to put them on the spot like this? It was cruel as well as being in downright bad taste. But an instant later, she forgave them. They were proud of their children and they were only wishing the same happiness for their friends. They had no idea that things weren't what they seemed between Brand and her.

Brand countered easily and calmly. "Trying to drum up business, old friend? Melody and I have a lot of getting reacquainted to do before we start having a family. Isn't that right, darling?"

"Right," she said curtly. "Nicole, how about a drink?" she asked in an effort to drop the distasteful subject. "I'm dying of thirst."

The entire evening was an ordeal. Brand stayed at her side almost constantly, calling her endearing names and treating her with such solicitous tenderness that the others could not possibly fail to get the implication that he was deeply in love with her. Melody hated the deception but she did not dare make it obvious. This was Brand's game and she had no choice but to play it by his rules.

After the first hour Tammy and Jim seemed to fare a little better, however. When the dog defected from him for a snooze on Tammy's lap, Jim went to sit down beside her, and after a few desultory false starts, they were soon talking about school and sports. Melody watched them without appearing to do so and was amazed to see the transformation that came over Tammy. The girl's face was aglow, with an inner light that had suddenly been turned on, and a genuine, unselfconscious smile came readily to her lips.

It was after eleven when they returned home. Tammy was almost friendly to Melody and Brand as they all trooped up the stairs to their rooms.

"Did you enjoy yourself, Tam?" Brand asked.

Tammy shrugged. "It wasn't so bad as I thought it would be," she admitted grudgingly. Then a smile flitted across her lips. "Yeah, I had a good time." She reached her room and opened the door, yawning. "Good night, Brand. 'Night, Melody."

Once they were in their own room, Brand repeated his question. "Did you have a good time as well?"

Melody shrugged and went across to the dresser, where she began removing her earrings. "It was all right, I suppose. I enjoyed seeing Nicole again."

"But?" He picked up instantly on what she had left unsaid and he came to stand just behind her so that their eyes met in the mirror.

Melody glared at him. "But I did not appreciate the loving act you put on," she snapped with spirit. "Darling this and darling that! Better watch it, Brand. Keep on laying it on so thick and someone is bound to suspect the truth."

"Which is?" he asked grimly.

Melody whirled to face him. "Which is that it's all one great big farce! I don't like playacting, deceiving people like this!"

"However," he said, echoing her thoughts earlier with such precision that she suspected he was a mindreader, "you don't have much choice, do you?"

Her shoulders hunched in defeat as she turned away from him. "No," she agreed hollowly. "I suppose I don't."

"Good," he said with a hint of granite, "so long as you realize that, we'll get along just fine."

She turned to look at him again and this time there was a question in her eyes. "Does it give you a sense of satisfaction to have such power over another human being?" she asked quietly. "Does it make you happy to know you can ruin someone else's life by ordering it to suit yourself?"

His eyes narrowed. "Is that what you believe?"

She nodded.

"Then there's nothing else to say, is there?" he returned. He walked swiftly to the door and went out of the room, leaving her to stare after him.

The headache of the evening before returned to nag at her again the next morning. Melody awoke earlier than usual, even before Brand, and she eased herself quietly from the bed and, carrying her clothes into the bathroom, dressed there. As she gulped down a couple of aspirins, she noticed how pale her face was. Constant tension was sapping her health as well as her looks, but there appeared nothing she could do about it except learn to cope better, because, as Brand had pointed out the night before, she was here to stay whether she liked it or not.

He was still asleep when she passed through the bedroom toward the door that opened onto the hall. No tension headaches to spoil his sleep, she thought bitterly.

It was both Juanita's and Opal's day off, so Melody went into the kitchen and made coffee herself. She carried her cup out to the patio. The hot sun felt soothing on her head and shoulders and slowly her muscles began to relax.

Ten minutes later she forced herself to get up and go inside. The only way there was going to be any breakfast was if she prepared it.

The food was almost ready when Brand, dressed in a pale-gray business suit, came into the kitchen. "How very wifely," he said with a hint of sarcasm. "Or did you cook only enough for yourself?"

"There's plenty," she said sharply, "if you want some."

He sat down and, as she laid a platter of bacon and eggs on the table, he looked up at her with a wry grin on his face. "What have you done, put arsenic in my share?"

"What an excellent idea!" she exclaimed. "I should have thought of that myself!"

"So that you could be free to return to your fiancé?" he asked swiftly.

It gave her great pleasure to smile sweetly and answer, "Of course. What else?"

His thick, dark brows lowered over his eyes like a thunderstorm swooping down over the earth. "You know that . . ."

Whatever he was going to say remained unsaid as Tammy entered the room, clad in her inevitable uniform of cut-off jean shorts and a T-shirt.

Melody was relieved. There had been black danger in Brand's eyes, as though perhaps she had gone beyond the limit with her taunting words, and she had been slightly alarmed. Brand had never been a man to allow anyone to push him too far, and she had come close to it just then.

"Bacon and eggs," she said to Tammy. "Are you hungry?"

Tammy glanced at the table and hesitated. "Fried. No," she said, shaking her head. "I think I'll boil an egg instead."

As she walked over to the cabinet to pull out a saucepan, Brand looked up at Melody, and this time there was a quizzical expression on his face instead of anger. She shook her head slightly and sat down, as surprised as he, but she was not about to ask any questions of Tammy until they were alone.

As soon as Brand had finished his breakfast, he left for the office. Melody and Tammy still remained at the table and Melody poured out another cup of coffee and picked up the morning *Caller*. "Did you get enough to eat, Tammy?" she asked as she unfolded the paper. "A boiled egg and a half a grapefruit doesn't go a long way."

"I've decided to go on a diet," the girl answered.

"I see," Melody murmured absently as she began to scan the headlines.

"Well," Tammy said bitingly, "aren't you going to gloat because I'm doing what you want?"

Melody shook her head. "There's no need to gloat, but I am pleased about your decision."

Later that morning she happened to walk past Tammy's opened bedroom, and as she glanced in she saw Tammy at the dresser, her face contorted, chewing her lip, as she attempted to wad her hair up onto her head.

Jim *had* got under the girl's skin! Melody smiled to herself, but carefully wiped it from her face before going into the room. "Practicing hairstyles?" she asked.

"Yes," Tammy scowled, "but all mine looks like is a rat's nest."

Melody laughed. "Can I help? When I was your age my girl friends and I used to spend hours at a time learning how to fix our hair."

For a minute she thought she would be refused. Tammy glared at her with dislike, but after a moment's hesitation she shrugged her shoulders and handed the comb to Melody. "I doubt if you can do anything," she said shortly. "It's too thick and straight."

"Let's see." Melody began to unpin the hair so that it fell around Tammy's shoulders, black as a moonless night.

She worked in silence for a little while as Tammy eyed

81

herself in the mirror. "What did you think of Jim?" Melody asked casually. "I liked him. Maybe we could invite him to dinner sometime soon."

"Not on your life!" Tammy said vehemently. "He'd only think I was chasing after him!"

"Oh, I don't think so," Melody answered. "After all, he's just visiting here and doesn't know any other teenagers yet. I'd think he'd be delighted if you invited him over."

"No, thanks." Tammy shook her head, causing Melody to lose her grip on a strand she was trying to pin up so that she had to begin again.

"Well, how about inviting some of your girl friends over then? I suggested it once and . . ."

"And I told you I didn't have any friends," Tammy hissed. "How many times do I have to tell you?"

Melody refused to allow Tammy's attitude to ruffle her. "What about Kathy Elbert and Lana Yates?" she asked mildly. "You three used to be great friends."

"That was when we were *little* kids," Tammy snapped impatiently. "They wouldn't want anything to do with me now."

"Why not?"

"Why not?" Tammy glared at her. "They just wouldn't, that's all."

"Well, as Brand told you," Melody went on, "it's your own fault if you seem to have no friends. You've put people off by your rudeness. Besides, I'll bet you haven't even called Kathy or Lana and told them you're in town, have you? I bet if they knew they'd be over here as fast as lightning." She shrugged her shoulders, deciding she had said enough on the subject for now. "Well, how do you like it? Not bad for a first attempt, huh? But what you really need is an expert cut. We'll make you an appointment this week."

Tammy surveyed the upswept hair. It was pinned in a casual knot in the back, curling over a little at the top and at the sides. Permitting herself a tiny smile, she said, "It makes me look older, don't you think, Melody?"

Melody choked back a laugh and said soberly, "Oh, definitely. Years older."

That afternoon a truck arrived, delivering all of Melody's belongings that had been left in Dallas. As she unpacked her things, the import of what she had done really hit her hard. She had given up for good the hard-won independent life she had carved out for herself there and she was right back where she had started.

She glanced around the luxurious bedroom. It was three times the size of the bedroom in her apartment and light-years away from it when it came to the expense of the furnishings. On the modest salary she had earned as Rob's secretary, she had had to stretch each penny as far as possible. Now, once again, she could have anything, within reason, that money could buy, but it didn't mean a thing.

Her gaze happened to fall on the rings on her left hand as she was about to open one of the boxes the truck had brought. She paused, staring thoughtfully at the glittering diamond engagement ring, the slender gold wedding band. No, Brand's money, this house . . . none of it meant a thing to her. The only thing that had ever mattered had been Brand himself and the love they had shared. She sank listlessly onto the bed, still looking at the rings on her hand that bound her to him. They seemed to be mocking her . . . or were they instead trying to give her a silent message?

Was it possible, she asked herself now for the first time, for them to recapture the love, the sheer magic of it, that they had once had? She had thought it totally dead after five years of separation, but was it? Certainly their relationship had undergone a radical change. Now there was much hurt and bitterness flowing beneath the surface, yet not always. Whenever Brand made love to her there was still a raging fire burning in them both. It was as impossible for either of them to be sexually indifferent to each other as it was to live without a pulsating heart. But was that—physical magnetism—enough to satisfy either of them emotionally for the rest of their lives or was that aspect of their beings to be starved forever?

Wearily, she shook her head. She had no answer. She stood up and opened another box, this one filled with a miscellany of items. She reached inside and pulled out a small, framed painting of the sand dunes and the water at Padre Island. She had fallen in love with it years ago, and Brand had bought it for her. After the divorce, when he had sent on the personal effects she had left behind, the painting had been included. She had kept it, she had assured herself, merely because she liked the painting and loved the island, but the truth was she had kept it because it had been a gift from Brand.

The telephone jangled, interrupting her thoughts, and remembering that Opal was off today, she laid the painting on the bed, reached across to the bedside table, and picked up the receiver.

"Hello, this is Lorraine White," the voice said crisply.

Melody froze. What now, she wondered, as she waited for the flow of abusive words she had come to expect from Lorraine. "Yes?"

"I'm calling for Brand, who is busy in a meeting. He wants me to tell you that he has a business dinner tonight and won't be home until late."

There was a jubilant, rather excited note to Lorraine's voice, and Melody was suddenly ill as the truth assaulted her with the violence of a hurricane. She licked her dry lips and said, with an outward calmness that made her proud, "I see. Thank you for the message. Good-bye, Lorraine." She hung up quickly before the secretary could have a chance to add anything more, and it was just as well because by then she was trembling and her throat was choked so that she would not have been able to continue the conversation without giving herself away.

Brand had no business meeting tonight at all! He was

spending it with Lorraine. She was positive of that. Why else had Lorraine sounded so triumphant?

Impotent rage surged through her. Brand was deliberately breaking his pact with her. He had found himself unable to stay away from Lorraine after all and he wasn't in the least concerned with her feelings about it . . . just as he hadn't been five years before. How she detested him for humiliating her like this! It was all so degrading and she was helpless to run away as she had before.

As if to reinforce her commitment, Dale dropped by that evening and had dinner with her and Tammy. When Melody told him Brand was at a business dinner it excited no interest from him whatsoever. She wondered if Dale knew about Brand and Lorraine and decided he probably did. But being a man as well as Brand's employee, he was hardly likely to tell her, especially since it was on his account that she was now married to Brand again.

Dale did not linger long after dinner, and really, Melody could not blame him. She was in a rotten mood and no fit company for anyone. Even Tammy seemed to come out of her own sulks long enough to look at her curiously at dinner when she happened to speak somewhat sharply in answer to one of Dale's questions. But she could not seem to help herself. As the hours passed, the angrier she became that Brand would dare to treat her to a repeat of this whole sordid business.

It was quite late when Brand came home. Melody was propped up in bed with a book. Though she had opened it over an hour before, she had not read two full pages.

Brand was surprised to see her awake. "Were you waiting up for me?" he asked. "You shouldn't have."

"Oh, I know that!" she said scathingly. "You'd much rather I didn't know how late you are or where you've been!"

"What are you talking about?" he asked sharply as he shed his jacket and began tugging at his tie.

He looked tired and sleepy and slightly irritable himself. Had Lorraine given him a hard time tonight, she wondered grimly. "I'm talking about your evening out," she said in a rising voice. "And making me look like a fool!"

Now Brand's voice was as cold as ice cubes. "Just how did I manage to do that?"

"Breaking our pact! You said we'd be faithful to each other, but you never meant to keep that promise at all, did you?" she asked bitterly.

His dark eyes glittered with his own anger now. "Are you accusing me of having been out with another woman tonight?" he demanded bluntly.

"I *know* you were!" she exclaimed.

"Didn't Lorraine call and tell you I had a business appointment?"

"Oh, yes!" she answered with a sneer on her face. "Did you really expect me to believe it, Brand? Do you really think I'm that naïve?"

He glared at her for a long time without speaking. Then he slowly began to unbutton his shirt. "Quite frankly," he said in a tired voice, "at this point I don't much care what you believe, Melody."

Her eyes widened. "You're not going to deny it then?" she asked tautly.

Brand shook his head. "No, I'm not going to deny anything." He stripped off his shirt and went into the bathroom, firmly shutting the door behind him.

Chapter Seven

"Wake up, sleepyhead. You're going to roast!"

Melody unwound her arms from beneath her head and rolled over onto her back. She opened her eyes and squinted from the glare of the blazing sun. Nicole, looking a frivolous seventeen in her tomato-red bikini instead of like a competent mother of two, loomed above her, laughing as her sons gleefully sloshed a pail of saltwater over Melody's feet.

Melody sat upright. "Hey, guys, no fair!" she protested to the giggling youngsters. "I'll get you back for that! I'll bury you in the sand!"

"Me!" Jason squealed with delight.

"No! Me!" Tommy shouted. "I'm the biggest. Bury me!"

Melody looked up at Nicole, who was by now convulsed with laughter. "You've got weird kids," she said. "I can't even scare them with threats."

"Not that kind, for sure," Nicole agreed. "They have a sandpile at home, you see, and that's one of their favorite games."

"Humph!" Melody got to her feet to the tune of the boys' insistence that she carry through her threat, and only after she had satisfied them that before the day was over she would "bury" them, did they finally wander off to play in a small, shallow pool near the water's edge.

This stretch of Padre Island was deserted and peaceful, for it was only accessible to four-wheel-drive vehicles, unlike the park areas. They had been here since early morning and only two or three other vehicles had passed by them. The only sounds at all were the everlasting cries of the sea gulls, the roar of the Gulf of Mexico, and the playful squeals of Nicole's children.

"Where is everybody else?" Melody asked as she picked up her now wet beach towel and vigorously shook as much sand off it as possible. Her gaze surveyed the water, searching for heads bobbing in the foaming waves, and, finding none, swept over the endless stretch of beach.

"Carl and Brand went to gather firewood," Nicole answered, "and Jim and Tammy went hunting for shells."

Together they moved at a leisurely pace toward the two jeeps that were parked a few yards away. The men had rigged up a tarpaulin covering the jeeps so that it afforded a large, shaded area, and beneath it were the ice chests and folding chairs they had brought along.

They had just opened canned Cokes and sat down in the

chairs when the two men topped one of the sand dunes and began the downward trek, their arms loaded with driftwood. Melody could not help but notice how magnificent Brand appeared, with his broad, bare shoulders and chest darkened by the sun and his long, lean legs tapering down from his blue swim trunks.

As they approached, she looked away, toward the water, hurt squeezing her throat. The last time they had been with the Simons she had been angry with Brand for overplaying the loving husband angle, but her embarrassment then was nothing compared to what she was experiencing today. This time he was ignoring her with icy contempt, and she was sure that Nicole and Carl could not have failed to notice it. That was why she had stretched out on the beach towel for such a long time, feigning sleep. It seemed easier than pretending she was having a good time.

"Hey, Mommy, come see what we made!" Tommy shouted.

Nicole sighed. "I knew I wouldn't get to sit still for long," she said as she got up and went toward the boys.

"How about opening us a couple of beers, Melody?" Carl asked as he dumped his pile of wood near the fire hole Brand had dug earlier.

"Sure." She went at once to the ice chest and a moment later left the shade to join them.

Carl took his with an absent "Thanks" and, murmuring something about matches, went toward his jeep. Melody handed Brand his beer and their fingers accidentally touched.

She removed her hand quickly and he gave a bitter smile. "You can't stand to touch me, can you?"

She shivered, although the hot, relentless sun beating down on her skin was scorching. "You can't stand to behave civilly to me, can you?" she retorted.

His eyebrows shot upward with a question. "Have I been rude?"

"Damn you, you know what you're doing!" She struggled to keep her voice low and controlled. "You're being so polite you might as well come right out and shout to everyone how much you detest me!"

His black eyes flickered over her face and then slowly his gaze traveled downward to the bare expanse of honey-golden skin that was broken only by the white strips of her bikini. Melody's face went hot as he took his time looking her over before his eyes returned to a scrutiny of her face. "So you'd rather the 'loving' treatment after all, hmm?" he taunted. "I appreciate the offer, but with you dressed like that perhaps it's better if I keep my distance as long as others are around."

Her hands clenched at her sides and it was all she could do to keep herself from hitting him. *"That* wasn't what I meant and you know it!" she hissed. "You're being hateful just to punish me, but it won't work, Brand! Two can play your little game, and if you don't care what others think, then neither do I!" She whirled around and stalked toward the sand dunes, needing to get away from everyone until she had a tight grip on her emotions.

The entire past week had been this way, ever since the night she had accused him of being out with another woman. Not once in that time had Brand so much as smiled at her. He was remote and cold every occasion they met, which had been seldom. Although they still shared a bed, at no time had he approached her and for that, at least, she had been grateful. It was an intolerable enough situation as it was, having to live with him and sleep in his bed, but she knew if he had tried to make love to her she would have behaved like a wildcat.

What she could not understand was why Brand was as angry with her as she was with him. She had been played for a fool, yet he acted as though he had been unjustly accused. But that was impossible. It had happened in the past and it had happened again—she had no doubts about that. She supposed, on reflection, that what he was really

89

angry about was the fact that she was on to him. He wanted everything his way and it had been no part of his plan for her to know the truth about his double life. But, then, he had no idea that she had known it all along.

Little Jason came running up to her, putting an end to her morose thoughts. "Come see what me 'n Tommy builded, Mel'dy," he urged excitedly.

She smiled at him. "All right. What is it?"

"It's a castle an' it's *real* big!" He stretched out his arms in an effort to show her the scope of its bigness, and together they made their way across the warm sand, their feet sinking into it, as they went to join the others.

Melody remained with the children the rest of the morning and by the time lunch was ready, Jim and Tammy had returned.

Melody was glad to see that Tammy, at least, seemed happier. She had not wanted to come on this outing and Melody suspected it was because she was disturbed over her looks in her new bathing suit and had not wanted Jim to see her in it. But once again Brand had taken control and ordered her to come along, claiming it was a family outing and it would not be right for her to stay alone at home. Now Tammy, in a dark navy-blue one-piece swimsuit, knelt on the sand and displayed for Tommy and Jason the shells they had picked up on their walk. Jim knelt beside her and they cheerfully allowed the boys to choose several sand dollars to keep for themselves.

Lunch was grilled hamburgers with potato chips, olives, cookies, and Cokes. Everyone crowded beneath the shade of the tarpaulin to eat, as the jeep blocked the gusty Gulf winds. Melody sat as far from Brand as possible and not once did she so much as look toward him. She was beyond the point of caring anymore whether Carl and Nicole saw through their act. What did it matter, anyway?

Afterward, while Nicole, Tammy, and Melody cleared away the clutter, Carl and Brand spread a blanket on the shady ground for Tommy and Jason. The two boys grumbled about the necessity for naps, but their father was adamant and in only a short time they were both sound asleep.

Nicole and Carl decided to take a short walk while they had the freedom to be alone and Melody promised to stay in sight of the boys while they did so. She took her beach towel, suntan lotion, and a thick mystery novel and went out to sun bathe again. Tammy and Jim headed off in the direction of the sand dunes, carrying along a transistor radio. Brand went off for a solitary walk along the shoreline in the opposite direction of Carl and Nicole.

An hour later, the boys were awake and Melody was busily fulfilling her promise by "burying" them. Tommy was already covered with sand from his feet to his neck, but he was quickly coming unstuck as he squirmed to watch Melody do the same thing to his brother.

"Need some help?"

Melody paused to glance up at Brand, who stood looming over them. He was smiling at Jason and then his gaze went to her face. She was glad she wore her sunglasses. They seemed to offer some measure of protection from him. She shrugged indifferently. "Suit yourself," she said ungraciously.

"Yeah," Tommy insisted. "Do me again! I'm comin' all undone!"

Brand laughed and knelt. "That's because you're a wiggle-worm," he told him.

Carl and Nicole came back a short time later and flopped beside them. By this time the boys' energy was too much to allow them to remain still any longer and they scattered sand from their small bodies the way a dog does water when its fur is wet.

"Help me build a castle," Tommy pleaded to his father.

"You built one this morning," Carl reminded him.

"We want a bigger one, don't we, Jason?"

Melody stood up and quietly left the little group, going toward the Gulf. She waded in cautiously, bending now

91

and then to scoop up water to slosh over her legs and arms. When she was about waist deep, she sat down, allowing the buoyant waves to wash over her and shove her where they might.

She could see the others still on the shore. The distance made them appear small. The current had pushed her away so that they were now to her left instead of directly in front of her.

Melody turned her back to the beach, deciding to go farther out. She had always enjoyed riding the really big waves. When she was about to crest she would calculate it to the split second and when it came crashing down she would jump up and let the force of the water thrust her forward like hapless flotsam.

She had no idea how long she played the game. Every few waves would push her back into relatively shallow water and she would begin the tiring trek out to the deep again.

The last time she went deeper than she had meant to and a sudden undercurrent began to drag at her legs. Panic seized her and she thrashed wildly against the powerful waves that crashed down upon her. Her head went underwater and she came up gasping for air only to swallow a mouthful of saltwater before being submerged by yet another foamy wave.

Two strong arms suddenly clamped around her and began towing her toward a sand bar. Melody sputtered and gasped for breath, and this time pure air entered her lungs. A moment later her feet dragged bottom and she was able to stand up in the waist-deep water.

Brand's grim face peered down at hers as he too gasped for breath. "Are you all right?"

She nodded and pushed wet, tangled hair from her face. "Yes," she gulped. "How . . . how did you get here in time? The undertow . . ." Her voice trailed off as the enormity of what almost happened suddenly hit her.

"I'd been watching you going deeper and deeper and I

had already started swimming out to you when I realized you were really in trouble. What the hell were you doing?" he demanded now, with violent fury. "Were you *trying* to drown yourself?"

"What difference would it make to you?" she snapped back, instantly forgetting the gratitude she had felt toward him only a moment before.

"Plenty," he growled in a deep voice. "It would be highly inconvenient to hold that dinner party we have planned for Friday night if you killed yourself . . . besides which it would leave me without a hostess!"

They glared at one another as the waves relentlessly pushed and shoved and tugged so that their bodies swayed toward each other. Melody thrust out a hand to keep from tumbling against him, and as she did his hand came up to grasp it. And all at once they were both laughing.

Brand's arms went around her, pulling her wet body against his. Then his salt-flavored lips came down to touch hers and they were infinitely warm and gentle and somehow comforting.

"Come on," he said softly, as his arms dropped away but he took one of her hands firmly in his, "let's go back. You've had enough swimming for a while."

The remainder of the day Brand was warm and friendly to her and Melody discovered that, despite their differences and the problems that remained between them, she far preferred him like this than distant and unapproachable. It was as though the past week had been a cold winter and she was only now emerging from it into the summer sun.

A week later, she stood in the tiled hallway beside Brand as they greeted their dinner guests. Melody's floor-length dress was black with wide straps that curved up from her breasts to clasp around her neck, leaving her shoulders and back bare. Her hair was swept into curls atop her head, a flame of fire to contrast brilliantly with her tanned skin and the stark black of the dress. Brand was impeccable in his dark suit and tie as he offered firm handshakes to the men and light kisses on the cheeks to most of the women.

They had invited around forty guests for the buffet dinner. Most of them Melody had already met, but there were a few business acquaintances Brand had included who were new to her. Melody hid her nervousness at being "on display" behind a welcoming smile and warm words, and before long she was so engrossed in seeing that her guests were comfortable, supplied with drinks, and congenial conversation that she forgot herself.

Juanita, with assistance from Opal and Melody both, had outdone herself with the food. There were slices of ham, beef tips in red wine sauce, chilled shrimp to be eaten with a variety of dips, vegetable dishes, and even some of Juanita's best tamales and enchiladas. There was also a tempting selection of desserts, and Melody smiled with pleasure at the compliments she received.

Although she had little time to spend with them, she was glad that Carl, Nicole, and Dale were among the guests. Their supportive presence aided the self-confidence she needed because they all did their best to circulate and keep conversation flowing smoothly.

Dale had brought along a date, a woman named Marie, whose last name escaped Melody. After everyone had been served, she saw the two of them seated together on the patio, where many of the guests milled around in the warm, evening air. Melody had a free moment, so she joined them.

"Great party, Mel," Dale told her.

"Thanks," she said easily as she dropped into a chair beside them. "You've both been a big help, moving around and talking to people like you have."

"Oh, Marie here is a good circulator," Dale said with a teasing grin. "That's why it's taken me months to get a date with her."

Marie's face reddened slightly. She smiled at Melody.

94

"He's exaggerating, It's just that I'm so busy with my job that I don't have much time for dates."

"What is your job?" Melody asked curiously.

"I'm a nurse," came the surprising reply. "A private one, so my hours are often erratic."

Melody happened to glance at her brother and amazement shot through her. She had seen him with many different women in the past, but the tender expression on his face as he watched the woman at his side was something entirely new. Devil-may-care Dale falling for a nurse! It was incredible.

Someone called Dale away just then, so Melody spent the next five or ten minutes alone with Marie, and she quickly discovered the reason why her brother was drawn to the girl. She was in no way a beauty, with short dark hair and unremarkable features, but there was a certain glow about her that created a beauty far deeper than the surface. She had an unaffected warmth and friendliness coupled with a quiet self-confidence that encouraged a like response from all she met. Yes, Melody could easily see what Dale liked in Marie. Her patients probably adored her as well.

Dale returned to them and Melody stood up, smiling. "I'd better get back to my other guests. Marie, you must let Dale bring you to dinner sometime so that we can get better acquainted."

She moved away from them and was just about to reenter the house when she met Lorraine. So far, beyond a polite greeting when she had arrived, they had not spoken to each other.

Lorraine was breathtakingly lovely tonight in a sheer, flowing dress of lavender and white. The scent of her perfume wafted on the night air like a flower garden.

Melody mustered a friendly smile. "I hope you're enjoying yourself, Lorraine. May I get you another drink?" she asked, indicating the nearly empty glass the other woman held.

"I know where the bar is," Lorraine said abruptly, "and I've never stood on ceremony in this house."

"That's fine," Melody said easily, refusing to allow herself to become upset.

She was about to move on when Lorraine halted her. "Tonight won't change anything, you know," she said in a low voice.

"What do you mean?"

"I mean this party," Lorraine said. Her eyes flashed. "You're doing this to insinuate yourself back into Brand's social life . . . to get people to accept you again as his wife. But it won't work. People are feeling sorry for Brand, did you know that?" she asked maliciously. "They think you somehow pressured him into taking you back again!"

Melody tensed. *Was* that what everyone was saying? And how ironic if it was true! It was hilarious, really, but for some strange reason she did not find it very funny.

With a supreme effort of will, Melody forced another smile to her lips. "I can't help what people say or think, Lorraine," she said with a tiny shrug. "It's strange the odd notions people get in their heads sometimes, isn't it? Now," she added with a calmness she was far from feeling, "if you'll excuse me, I need to see to my other guests."

With a pleasant nod, she walked away, but not before she had time to see the disbelief on Lorraine's face. She smiled grimly to herself as she stepped into the house. In the past Lorraine had often made her feel inadequate and awkward in social situations such as this, with sharp little comments about her dress or the menu, and Melody had taken it all to heart, feeling herself a failure to Brand. This time she was older, more mature, and she had no doubts at all about the success of the party or her dress and Lorraine had realized it. That was why she had attacked her instead on a more personal level.

Was it true, she wondered again, that people were talking about Brand and her as Lorraine said? It could be, but then, considering the source, it could just as easily be untrue. With an inward shrug, she dismissed it from her mind. It really didn't matter one way or another.

What did matter, however, was seeing Brand and Lorraine together a half hour later. They were standing near the fireplace in the living room, engrossed in each other, and when Melody saw them something stabbed her heart. Lorraine's face was tipped up as she smiled while Brand's dark head was bent down over hers as he spoke to her. They were as oblivious to all the others in the room as though they were completely isolated and alone.

Melody's hands knotted at her side and she turned away abruptly. She could not bear to see them together like that, and waves of humiliation washed over her as she realized that all their guests were also treated to the sight. *I do not care,* she told herself fiercely. *I do not care.* All that remained was to convince herself of it.

By the time the last of the guests had gone, the strain of the long evening had taken its toll. Melody was exhausted, yet her taut nerves told her it would be hours before she could relax enough to sleep.

Unexpectedly, Brand draped a casual arm across her shoulders as they climbed the stairs together. "I'd say it was a successful party, wouldn't you?" he asked, smiling down at her.

Melody wanted to jerk away from his touch. He had paid open attention to Lorraine tonight and yet now he was acting just as though nothing had happened. But, listlessly, she let his arm remain where it was. What was the use, she asked herself dully, in starting another fight? If she did, she would have to name Lorraine and bring the whole affair to a head . . . and then what? She would still be Brand's wife. She could not leave no matter what the cost to her pride. Now she swallowed hard over the lump of bitter despair that lodged in her throat and her voice was husky as she responded to his casual question. "Yes, it was. I think everyone had a good time."

His hand gave her shoulder a tiny squeeze as they

reached their room and went inside. "Of course they did. You were the perfect hostess and I received many compliments on my beautiful wife."

Now she was able to leave the curve of his arm without making it obvious. She went to the dresser and began to unpin her hair. It fell, like billowing waves of fire, against her shoulders. "I suppose we're still a subject for gossip," she said, and her voice slightly hardened as she recalled Lorraine's poisonous words. "I mean, our getting married again."

Brand laughed as he shed his jacket and opened his shirt, revealing his hair-darkened chest. "Oh, sure. That's only to be expected. I was told a number of times that I showed remarkable good sense in winning you a second time."

Winning! Melody laughed aloud. "What a strange word to use for blackmail!"

Brand's smile vanished. "I've heard that word from you enough," he said in a voice of steel. "You are not to use it again!"

"What?" Melody taunted. "Does the truth bother you?"

Brand strode forward swiftly and his face was dark and angry as he grabbed her shoulders and shook her. "No," he growled in a low voice. "The truth doesn't bother me, but it does bother you. Why won't you tell me why you ran out on me five years ago?"

She closed her eyes against him, trying to shut out her acute awareness of him. "Answer me!" he insisted, and when she mutely shook her head, he jerked her in his arms and his lips came down to cover hers in ruthless punishment.

She tried to fight him but the strength of his arms imprisoned her as his lips stormed her face and throat. Although she tried to resist him, the fire of his kisses began to ignite an answering fire in herself. Her skin was hot and flushed as it awakened to a need that only he could satisfy. Her hands, which had been beating against him, fluttered, went still for an instant and then began a sensitive exploration of his bare chest and back.

Brand groaned and, lifting her in his arms, carried her to the bed, and now she had no will left with which to fight him. Every nerve of her body ached for his touch, clamored for the heights of ecstasy, in sure knowledge that the passion he aroused in her only he could quench. As he unclasped the straps of her dress from around her neck and began to shove the offending cloth away from her breasts, she gave a tiny sigh of pure desire and Brand groaned again. "Oh, Melody," he whispered thickly, "you always did drive me to distraction."

A half hour later, in contented lethargy, they smiled at each other as their heads nestled close upon the pillows. Brand's fingers intertwined with hers. "Tell me," he demanded huskily, *at this moment* are you glad or sorry I blackmailed you into coming back?"

"At this moment?" she asked. Her heart thudded as her senses drank in the nearness of him. She was quiveringly alert to the warmth of his body, the strength of the hand that clasped hers, and his face with lips softened by her kisses and eyes that seemed to melt her with an incredible tenderness. In that instant she could deny him nothing and she did not attempt to prevaricate. "At this moment," she repeated slowly, "I'm glad, Brand."

He nodded with a satisfied smile. "Then there may be hope for us yet," he murmured.

"What do you mean?"

Now he shook his head. "Nothing," he said easily, "except that it's far more pleasant like this than when we're fighting, don't you agree?" He turned over and reached for the switch on the bedside lamp. An instant later the room was plunged into darkness.

His arm came across her waist as he settled his head against the pillow again. "It's been a long night," he said lazily against her ear. "Let's get some sleep."

"Yes," she agreed. "I'm glad we don't give parties every night." She yawned sleepily.

"It'll be a while before I have time to do much partying again," he said unexpectedly. "I'm going to have to make several business trips out of town in the near future."

Melody stiffened. "You're going to be away?" she asked blankly.

"Yes." His lips nibbled at her earlobe. "I'd like to take you along with me," he told her, "but you'd only be bored. Besides, I think Gram and Gramps have had enough of Tammy's company for a while, and we can't leave her here alone. You understand, don't you?"

"Oh, yes," she answered readily. "I understand." And indeed she did. They were right back to square one again. With icy coldness spreading slowly through her body, numbing her, she wondered whether Lorraine would be joining him out of town or whether there would be some other woman waiting for him instead.

In utter despair, she stared wide-eyed into the darkness of the night. She had thought she had built up strong defenses against Brand, but now she acknowledged to herself that he still had the power to hurt her . . . power he refused to relinquish. And the pain cut much deeper than a mere layer of pride.

Chapter Eight

"I'm sorry for you, Melody. I'm sorry for you, Melody. I'm sorry for you, Melody." Brand's words whirled around and around inside her head like the turning of the car wheels as Melody drove away from the airport.

She made a right onto the highway leading back toward the city. Tears filmed her eyes so that she had to brush them away in order to see. "I'm sorry for you, Melody." Well, so was she sorry for herself.

Her gaze lifted and she could see Brand's New York-bound plane in the distant sky. So far away from her so quickly! But, then, the two of them had been light-years apart for a long time now . . . five years to be exact.

It was three days since the party they had given and the night she had discovered he would be going away from her again, and during those days it had been impossible for her to completely hide her feelings. Toward Brand she was cool and remote, both unwilling and unable to respond to his smiles or his gentle teasings, so that she effectively wiped out the warmth and tenderness that had sprung up between them so briefly.

She had told herself repeatedly that she was behaving in a ridiculous manner. After all, Brand was merely going away on a business trip and it did not automatically follow that there would be another woman involved. Men who were faithful to their wives went away on business trips all the time. Yes, but they were not married to her, and what Brand had done once could easily be repeated.

He had no idea what had brought on her abrupt change of attitude, of course, and he had been furious because she refused to discuss with him what was bothering her. But her pride came to the fore again, preventing her from speaking out freely, isolating her with its cold protective shell.

As a result Brand had become withdrawn and quiet too, so that once more there was only that hated cold politeness between them. She knew that the change in her baffled him and possibly even hurt him, but she could not help herself. She was hurt as well and it was beyond her to pretend that nothing was wrong.

What had happened to her? she wondered. When Brand had first insisted she marry him again, she had felt nothing but contempt for him. At the time she had promised herself she would never allow the inner core of her being to be touched by him or Lorraine again, and for a while it had worked. But somehow Brand *had* reached in and contacted that deep, private essence of her once more, sliced it with the razor blade of sharp, emotional awareness, and left it raw and bleeding. Now she had to start all over again the long, tedious chore of trying to heal it.

Inside the airport Melody stood off to one side while Brand checked his bags and picked up his ticket. He was easily the most distinguished-looking man in the crowd around the ticket counter. His height compelled attention, since he seemed to dwarf the other men there, but it was more than that . . . it was the controlled dynamics of his personality that seemed to vibrate authority as well as magnetic, attractive masculinity. He was, Melody realized with a start, the sort of man who was admired by both sexes . . . the women for the sensuous aura that was as much a part of Brand as was breathing, the men because they recognized in him the successful, dominant traits they wanted for themselves.

She watched as Brand tucked his ticket into the breast pocket of his pale blue suit before he came to join her. He looked down at her without even the smallest hint of a smile. "There's no need," he told her in a metallic voice, "for you to bother seeing me off. It would just be a waste of time for the both of us and I've got some reports I need to look over."

She felt as though he had slapped her across the face and knew it was illogical, even crazy. Why should Brand want her to hang around when they were scarcely speaking? Yet logic did nothing to stop the flow of the hurt that was spreading through her like blood coursing from a punctured vein.

Melody was proud of the way she masked her feelings behind an indifferent shrug. "Okay," she said flippantly as she turned to leave him. "Have a nice trip."

She had only taken one step away when his hand shot out to grasp her wrist. As she looked up at him questioningly, there was a set, concrete hardness to his jaw. "You'd run away from me again if it weren't for Dale, wouldn't you?" he asked bluntly.

She wasn't expecting the probing question and it rocked

her off balance for a moment. Then she boldly met his eyes and nodded. "Yes," she admitted with stark frankness. "I would."

"Why?" Brand's tone was abrasive to her ears. "Still hankering over that guy in Dallas?" She tensed, not even daring to breathe, and when it was apparent that she was not going to answer the question, he went on brusquely, "I'm sorry for you, Melody. One minute you think you want that other man; the next you're in my arms and loving it despite the fact that you think you hate me. The truth is you're so confused you don't know what you want. But I'm not confused about what I want . . . or expect, and I'm fast losing patience with your vacillating emotional moods. You may as well resign yourself to the fact that you are my wife. I told you before that this marriage is going to work and I'm ready to be a generous and agreeable husband to you, but if you continue to cross me, you'll find me a dangerous enemy."

As she turned the car into the drive, she wondered just what it was that Brand did want and expect of her. It seemed as though he wanted her to accept his attention whenever he wished to give it to her, that he wanted her to play the part of happy, loving wife at all times, even in private, all the while leaving him free to pursue his own pleasures away from her whenever the mood struck him. Brand wanted it all his own way, but she could not go along with that. He had forced her to marry him again and he was still carrying on his extramarital affairs, and if he thought that added up to her behaving like a biddable wife, grateful for the few crumbs of tenderness he threw her, then he was much mistaken. He had told her once that he admired her spirit, and now her spirit rebelled at such mockery, and she knew that she would fight him every step of the way.

She decided, as she entered the house, that she would put Brand completely out of her mind, at least for a while. He would be gone probably a week and there was no sense in allowing herself to wallow in analytical thoughts of their farce of a marriage. Instead, she would concentrate on Tammy. The girl desperately needed the company of others of her own age, and as an idea occurred to her, Melody hurried upstairs to her bedroom and the telephone before she could change her mind.

A few minutes later, with a satisfied smile to her lips, she cradled the receiver and then went downstairs to the kitchen to have a private conversation with Juanita.

But the next afternoon, shortly before two o'clock, she was having second thoughts. What if Tammy was angry with her for her interference? What if she was rude and uncivil? As she lingered in the hallway, listening for the doorbell, she glanced through the glass door that opened onto the patio in the back. She could see Tammy there, curled up in a lounge chair with a paperback book. She was totally absorbed in her reading and Melody watched her anxiously, wishing she could read the girl's reaction from her profile.

Ten minutes later, the girls trooped through the front door. "Hi, Melody," greeted Lana Yates. "We're all here, as you can see."

Melody smiled warmly. Indeed they were, about ten of them. She had left it to Lana and Kathy Elbert to invite the other girls, girls who had known and liked Tammy in the past. Now they were all grinning with delight over their little secret. "I'm so glad to see you all, girls, and I know Tammy will be, too. I hope you brought your bathing suits along?"

"Yes. We each brought Tam a 'welcome home' gift, too," Kathy told her. "Where is she?" she ended eagerly.

Melody turned and pointed toward the patio. "Go on through, girls, and I'll be along shortly with some cold drinks for you."

She remained still, however, while the girls went out onto the patio. She had deliberately stayed behind, wanting to leave Tammy alone with her friends for the first few minutes so as not to interfere, but she could not help but watch her reception anxiously. What if she resented the fact that they were here?

Her anxiety did not last. She watched as Tammy, after one stunned moment, began to smile and hug the girls who had come to visit her. Melody sighed with relief, and until her muscles went limp, she had had no idea just how taut she had been.

She watched for an instant longer, and then she hurried to the kitchen.

"Well, how did it work?" Juanita asked pointedly.

"I think we did the right thing," Melody said with a delighted smile. "She seems glad to see them."

Juanita eyed her thoughtfully. "Maybe it was the right thing for you to come back home, too."

Melody froze. "Did you think it wasn't?"

Juanita shook her head as she went back to spreading chicken salad on slices of sandwich bread. "I just didn't know," she admitted honestly. "I was afraid you would hurt Mr. Brand and Tammy again."

Melody knotted her fists at her side and asked as calmly as possible, "And now?"

Juanita lifted her head and gave her one of her rare smiles. "Now I think maybe it's the best thing that could happen for all of you. This house has come alive again, like it was meant to be. For too long it's been like a big, silent tomb, what with Tammy off at one school or another and Mr. Brand hardly ever at home. That party you gave was the first party in this place since you went away, and even when Tammy was at home there were never any young people here to visit her. Yes," she added slowly, "maybe it's good you came back after all."

Melody wasn't so sure herself, but to change the subject, she asked, "What can I do to help here, Juanita? Are the sandwiches almost ready?"

"*Sí*," Juanita told her. "You can pour the soft drinks."

A few minutes later they carried the refreshments outside, and Melody remained to visit with the girls for a little while and to inspect Tammy's hoard of gifts—

perfume, necklaces, earrings, tiny stuffed animals. Tammy herself was like a different person, the girl she used to be so long ago, smiling and laughing and chattering just as fast as any of the others.

The girls stayed most of the afternoon. They swam and lazed around the pool, giggling and catching up on years of news. Melody saw that they were kept well supplied with snacks and cold drinks, but she did not remain to stifle the free flow of girlish confidences.

She was in her bedroom, lounging on the bed and flipping idly through a magazine, when Tammy came in unexpectedly. Melody threw a quick glance at the clock and saw that it was almost six. "Did everyone leave?" she asked.

Tammy nodded and dropped to the edge of the bed. "Yes. Tomorrow I'm invited to Kathy's for lunch and tomorrow night we're both invited to spend the night at Lana's house. Is it okay?"

"Sure," Melody agreed. "Well, did you enjoy yourself today?"

Tammy grinned at her. "You know I did." She looked down at her hands and mumbled, "Thanks for inviting them."

Melody smiled. "You're quite welcome, Tam. I'm just glad it worked out. I was afraid you'd be angry at me for doing it behind your back."

Tammy threw her a rueful glance. "I've been a pain all summer, haven't I?" she acknowledged suddenly.

Melody laughed and nodded. "Yes," she said honestly, "you have!"

"I'm sorry," Tammy mumbled as she again stared at her hands.

"Hey, it's all right," Melody told her. She reached over and covered Tammy's hands with her own. "I'd just like you to know that whenever you've got a problem or you're unhappy about something, I'm here to listen and to help, if possible."

Tammy grimaced. "Well, if that's the case, here's a problem. One of the girls, Jerrie Wharton, is having a party Friday night, . . . you know, a boy–girl date party. I'm invited, but I'd look dopey to show up without a date."

"Hmm," Melody murmured. "What about Jim Simon, then? Why don't you invite him to go with you?"

Tammy shook her head. "Oh, no, I couldn't ask a boy to be my *date!*" She sounded both scandalized and terrified.

"Under ordinary circumstances, I wouldn't want you to," Melody acknowledged, "but since you don't know any local boys who would like to take you and since Jim doesn't know many teenagers here, I think it would be a good idea. He'd probably love to go with you."

It took quite a bit of persuading, however, before Melody had convinced Tammy to call him, but when she did finally work up the courage, he accepted readily.

Melody thought Tammy was lovely in a new red-and-white sundress they bought for the party. As she watched her leave with Jim that Friday night, she felt a flicker of sisterly pride. True, Tammy was still a bit plump, but with her new haircut and the small amount of weight she had lost, she looked immensely prettier than she had at the beginning of the summer.

She waited up until Tammy came home that night, expecting to hear a repeat of the bubbly reports Tammy had given her the past few days about how much fun she was having with her renewed friendships, but it was a sulky, unhappy girl who returned to her.

"It was awful," she cried with despair. They were in Tammy's room, and as she kicked off shoes and began taking off her dress she added, "I'm ugly and fat and hopeless!"

Melody was shocked. "What on earth happened?"

"I thought Jim liked me, at least a little bit," she amended, "but he fell for one of the other girls there—Theresa Jennings. She's one of the prettiest girls in town, slim and small and with long blond hair. Not that I blame him!" she ended bitterly.

"Did Jim just desert you or what?" Melody demanded, trying to get to the bottom of the thing.

"Not exactly," Tammy conceded. "Oh, he was polite and spent most of the time with me, but he danced a few times with Theresa and I could just tell the way they were looking at each other. I felt like an idiot! I bet he's already asked her for a date! I hate Jim Simon!"

"I'm sure you're making it all out to be much worse than it was, but even if it's true, Tammy, he's not the only boy in the world. There are others, and you'll soon be meeting a lot of them, especially once school starts."

"I hate boys! I never want to see another one in my life!" Tammy blurted out roughly as she wiped a tear from her eye.

Melody was dismayed and soothed the girl the best she could. As she returned to her own bedroom a little later, she wished desperately that she could protect Tammy from hurts such as this, but the truth was that nobody could protect another from ever getting hurt, especially in the game of love—even puppy love. It was something everyone had to work out for themselves. Even so, she hoped that Tammy was mistaken about Jim. It wasn't that she wanted anything serious to develop between them—certainly not at their age—but just now, when Tammy was blossoming open into a lovely person again, she desperately needed the self-confidence that came with a close friendship with a boy.

The next day Tammy had reverted back to her old, sulky self, and when one of her girlfriends called to invite her to a movie she turned it down. She spent long hours in her room, emerging only late that afternoon to join Melody on the patio as they waited for dinner.

They sat for quite some time in silence, watching the bay below the bluff. Then, unexpectedly, Tammy asked, "Why did you leave Brand five years ago?"

Melody was startled. Although Tammy had resented her coming back initially, this was the first time the girl had ever questioned her about what had happened to make her leave in the first place.

Her gaze was riveted to the water as she answered stiltedly, "I . . . had my reasons, but I don't really care to go into it now."

"Why?" Tammy demanded. "Do you think I'm too young to understand?"

Slowly Melody turned to look at the girl and then she shook her head. "It's not that," she said gently. "But it's personal. It's not something I intend to discuss with anyone."

Tammy frowned. "Was it because of me?" she asked abruptly.

"No, of course not!" Melody cried vehemently. "Is that what you've thought all these years?"

Tammy nodded. "I thought maybe it was just that you didn't like having a kid to raise and . . ."

"Then you were wrong." Melody cut her off swiftly. "It had nothing at all to do with you, Tam, I swear! I love you very much. I always have!"

"Then if it wasn't me, it was something that went wrong between you and Brand?"

Melody nodded wearily.

Tammy's gaze returned to the water and her voice was stiff as she asked, "If that's so, then isn't it possible that whatever went wrong before can happen again and that you'll leave again? Do you love Brand, Melody? Is that why you came back?"

"Why all these questions all of a sudden?" Melody countered.

"Because I want to know."

"I'm sorry." Melody shook her head firmly. "My relationship with Brand is private and I won't discuss it, even with you, Tam."

"Then, like I said, it's possible you'll leave us again,

109

isn't it?" Tammy said in a harsh-sounding voice. "And I'll suddenly get shipped off to a boarding school somewhere again."

At that moment Dale walked through the doorway and both Melody and Tammy looked up to see him. At the sight of him Melody was forcibly reminded of the circumstances once more and she said quickly, in a low voice to Tammy, "Oh, no, I won't be leaving again. You can count on it."

Her definite assertion that she would not be leaving Tammy again seemed to be the magic words that put the girl at peace. During the next few days the two of them seemed to draw swiftly closer, and Melody was astounded at how much the girl opened up to her, talked to her and confided in her. It was as though she were starving for the security of a relationship with an adult woman that she had been missing since Melody had gone away all those years ago. Remorse over the pain she realized she must have unwittingly caused the young girl when she left filled Melody's heart so that she bent over backward to give Tammy all the attention she craved. There were so many years to make up for, and she was aware now in a way she had not been before that Tammy's troubled years had been directly her own fault because the child had thought she had been personally responsible for her leaving. It was something Melody felt a deep contrition about, and she only hoped and prayed she would never hurt anyone to such an extent again.

Several days later, Brand came home without warning. It was Opal's and Juanita's day off and Melody was in the process of dusting the living room furniture when she heard the front door opening. She didn't bother to look up, thinking it was Tammy coming home from an afternoon at Lana's, until he said quietly from behind her, "Hello."

Melody whirled, dust cloth in hand, her eyes wide with surprise. "Hello. I . . . I wasn't expecting you," she said lamely. She was amazed at her suddenly pounding heart, at how deeply glad she was to see him.

"Obviously not," he said with a slight smile. "Why are you cleaning house? I thought that was Opal's job?" He deposited his briefcase on the sofa and dropped his suitcase on the floor beside it.

She glanced down at the cloth she held and gave a small laugh. "It is, but it's Opal's day off, remember? Why didn't you telephone? I would have met your plane."

Brand shrugged and sank down onto the sofa, tugging his tie loose and opening the top button of his shirt. For the first time Melody became aware of how extremely tired he appeared. "I didn't see any point in bothering you," he said, "so I just took a cab."

"How was your trip?" she asked diffidently. "You never called."

He glanced up at her then and his eyes were piercing. "The trip was successful, I suppose you could say. As to my not calling—well, you didn't bother to call me either."

No, she hadn't. She had not wanted to go through the torture of perhaps discovering him with another woman again, but she could hardly point that out. "I . . . you must be thirsty," she said quickly. "I'll make you a drink and then I'll get some dinner started."

"Wait!" As she began to move away, he halted her. When she looked back at him, he was struggling to his feet and his hand was in his coat pocket. "I brought you something," he said as he extracted a small package.

"You shouldn't . . . I didn't expect a gift, Brand," she stammered in confusion.

"No?" His voice was quizzical. "I always brought you gifts from my other business trips."

"Yes," she acknowledged, "but that was . . . well, that was different."

"Agreed," he said drily, "but nevertheless this is for you."

She took the box from him but her fingers were slow and hesitant as she opened it. At last she lifted the lid and inside was an exquisite necklace—a small golden chain, dangling from it a small letter *M* fashioned out of diamonds.

"It's lovely!" she gasped. She raised her eyes to look at him. "Brand, it's beautiful, but it's too much. I . . ."

"Do you like it?" he cut off her words almost impatiently.

"Of course I do!" she exclaimed. "But . . ."

"No buts, then," he said softly. "Here, I'll put it on for you." He took the delicate chain from the box and clasped it around her neck.

Melody's skin tingled at his touch, and when he was done she turned, almost shyly, to face him. "Thank you," she said softly. "Thank you very much."

"Is that all I get for it?" Brand demanded with a hint of laughter in his voice and a bit of the old teasing twinkle in his eyes.

Melody laughed, breath catching in her throat as they looked at one another. And then, obediently, she raised on her tiptoes and kissed him. Brand's strong arms went around her waist, holding her tightly to him as Melody surrendered to the delight his touch always brought to her. Gone in a flash was the memory of the hostilities that had been between them, the long, empty hours while he had been away and had not called. There was now only this trembling, throbbing awareness of him.

When they drew apart at last, they were both smiling. A moment later, Melody ordered in a shaky voice, "Now, you sit down and relax while I get you a drink."

When she returned with his Scotch and water, he asked, "Where is Tam? Sulking in her room as usual?"

"Indeed not!" she exclaimed, and proceeded to outline the sneak party she had thrown and how involved Tammy now was with her friends. The only thing she did not mention was the fiasco over Jim. That was "girl talk," and unless Tammy wished to discuss it with Brand herself she felt it was a confidence.

Brand's face was a mixture of amazement and disbelief.

112

"You mean you've actually got her involved with kids her own age again? My darling, you are an absolute miracle worker!"

My darling! Melody felt a warm glow at the words, although in truth Brand looked so exhausted she was not sure he was even aware he had said it, much less meant it. After a few more minutes of talk, she stood up, saying, "I'm going to get dinner."

"Hmm, yes, I am hungry," Brand admitted. Then he yawned.

"Would you rather take a short nap first?" she asked. "I could delay dinner for an hour or so if you'd like to rest for a while."

Brand drained off his drink and stood up once again. He shook his head. "No, I don't have time for that. I want to call Lorraine and then I have some papers to study."

Depression settled over Melody like a heavy rain cloud. Lorraine again! As she made her way toward the kitchen, she had to fight hard to keep tears at bay. Brand had come home ready to be friendly again. He had even bought her an exquisite gift, but essentially nothing had changed.

As she entered the kitchen, she wondered dully what kind of a gift Brand had brought home for his secretary. And why, she asked herself in a blaze of sudden fury, should she even care? Brand meant nothing to her anymore, and nothing he did could ever have the power to hurt her again. Only fools played with fire twice.

Chapter Nine

"Telephone, Tammy!" Melody called out from the kitchen doorway. Tammy was sitting at the table drinking a Coke and chatting with Juanita while she peeled potatoes for dinner, but she rose at once.

"Is it Kathy?" she asked. "She's already called three times today."

Melody shook her head. "I don't know who it is. Opal

answered the phone. What could be so important for Kathy to call about that many times in one day?" she asked with amused curiosity.

Tammy shrugged. "She's all upset because her family is leaving for a two-week vacation tomorrow and she doesn't want to go but her folks are making her. Can't say I blame her. They're going to visit relatives and they all have little kids. What a drag!" She passed through the doorway and headed for the telephone in Brand's study.

Melody grinned to herself at such dire problems as family vacations and retraced her way back to the living room where she had been arranging some cut flowers in a vase.

A moment later Tammy stormed into the room, her face red with indignation, her chest heaving, and her hands knotting and unknotting at her sides. Melody stared at her in alarm. "What's the matter?" she gasped.

"That . . . that Jim Simon is what's the matter!" the girl hissed through clenched teeth.

"Was that who called?"

Tammy nodded. "Yes. He had the nerve to ask me to go to the movies with him tonight!"

"But . . . I don't understand," Melody said slowly. "What's so dreadful about that?"

Tammy shot her an impatient look. "Don't you understand anything, Mel? I *told* you how he kept watching Theresa that night at the party, and he hasn't bothered to call me since then. But I *know* what happened! He asked Theresa for a date first but when she turned him down he decided to call poor little Tammy and give her a thrill! Well, I'm not going to be second choice with anyone, *especially* Jim Simon! He's a jerk!"

Melody was bemused by the angry tirade. Trying to sort out the facts, she asked in a calm voice, "How do you know he invited Theresa first? Did someone tell you so?"

Tammy's lips twisted with scorn. "Nobody had to tell me. I'm not stupid, you know! I'll bet he's been seeing her for the past week and she suddenly dumped him for

114

somebody else so now he figures he's bored enough to call me, but he won't be bothering me again. I made sure of that!"

"What did you say to him?" Melody asked with sudden trepidation. Tammy, she already knew to her cost, could be extremely rude when she was in one of her moods.

"I told him to drop dead," Tammy said with a satisfied smirk on her face. "I told him I couldn't stand him, that the only reason I'd been friendly to him in the first place was because you and Brand had ordered me to, but that I was sick and tired of him and that I never wanted to see him again!"

Melody sucked in a sharp breath. "Tammy! You didn't!"

"Yes, I did, and I'm glad, so there!" she answered, tilting her head back with a defiant gesture.

Melody closed her eyes for an instant, sighed deeply, then looked at Tammy directly. "The reason," she said quietly, "that Jim hasn't called you this past week is because his grandfather died suddenly and he had to fly to Iowa for the funeral."

Tammy's mouth formed a startled O and the livid color in her cheeks drained away. "How do you know?" she asked hoarsely.

"Nicole told me. He just got back yesterday. Now, don't you think you should call him back and apologize?"

Tammy shook her head. "I couldn't," she whispered as tears filmed her eyes. "I couldn't! Oh, Melody, you don't know how horrible I was to him!"

Melody smiled gently. "Oh, yes, I do, if you actually told him all those things you just said you did." She shook her head. "You've simply got to get a better grip on your temper, Tam. But first you must call Jim and at least try to make your peace with him."

"No." Tammy's voice was shaky. "I can't. Not ever!" She choked on a sob and, turning abruptly, rushed from the room.

Melody sighed again and sank to the edge of the sofa.

Poor Tammy, she thought. And poor Jim. What an awful mess! She wished she could call the boy herself and explain, but it would only make things worse. In order to do that she would have to reveal just how much Tammy really liked him and just how vulnerable she had been that night of the party, and she couldn't betray her that way.

At dinner that evening Tammy merely picked at the food on her plate. Her face was still pale and Melody could see that during the hours the girl had been alone in her room there had been a storm of tears.

Several times Brand glanced curiously at his sister, and finally he asked, "You're not eating very much tonight, Tam. Are you getting sick?"

Tammy shrugged. "I'm okay," she mumbled as she hunched over her plate.

Brand raised his eyebrows and looked questioningly at Melody, but she shook her head. "It's probably just the weather," she ventured, trying to smooth it over with some sort of explanation. "It's been so hot lately I don't have much appetite myself, and Tammy's been out in the sun often the past few days."

"Hmm," Brand uttered in a doubtful tone, but fortunately he did not pursue it. As he took a roll from the bread basket and began to butter it, he said, "Carl called me today to see about getting up a golf game in the morning, but I have to work."

"You don't usually work on Saturdays," Melody pointed out. "I wish you would get out with him, Brand. You've been looking too tired ever since you came back from your trip."

"A little wifely concern for my health and welfare?" he asked. The smile that played across his lips was grim.

Melody flushed and quickly picked up her water glass in an attempt to cover her embarrassment. It was true that Brand had pushed himself too hard the past few days, working long hours at the office each day and even more long hours in his study at home each evening. Melody had scarcely seen him, and tonight the dark circles beneath his eyes from lack of rest had prompted her to speak out. But now she wished fervently that she had kept quiet. She threw a concerned glance at Tammy to see whether she had been aware of the sarcasm in Brand's words, but apparently she had not because she was still glaring stonily at her plate.

"I appreciate your concern," Brand added now when it became obvious to him that Melody was not going to respond to his barbed comment, "but I still have a few things to catch up on at the office. However, I'm not planning to work tomorrow afternoon, so I thought we might invite Carl and Nicole over for a visit tomorrow if that's agreeable with you?"

"Certainly," she answered.

"It really has been a hellish week," Brand went on. "At this point I could use a vacation. Say," he exclaimed with sudden enthusiasm, "why don't we go to Rockport Sunday and take Gramps's boat out for a little fishing?"

"Sounds fine to me," Melody nodded. "What about you, Tam?"

"You could invite Carl's nephew along, too, if you like," Brand told her. "I'll bet he'd enjoy it."

Tammy lifted her head, promptly burst into tears, and, shoving back her chair, rushed from the room.

Brand could not have been more shocked if Tammy had hit him and the surprised expression on his face might have been laughable, Melody thought, if the circumstances hadn't been so upsetting.

"What did I do?" he asked in an amazed voice.

Melody shook her head and gave him a wry smile. "You said exactly the wrong thing at the wrong time. You mentioned Jim."

His eyes widened. "I thought I had hit upon a good idea, but obviously it wasn't," he said drily. "Better tell me the whole story."

Her own appetite gone now, Melody put her fork on

her plate and proceeded to outline what had happened. She tried to gloss over the true extent of Tammy's rudeness to the boy, but Brand knew his own sister even better than she, and when she had finished he leaned back in his chair and demanded, "So Tammy was inexcusably rude to Jim?"

"I . . . I guess you could say so," she acknowledged hesitantly, not liking the dark anger on his face. "But there were reasons, and . . ."

"No," Brand interrupted. "There's never a reason to be quite so rude as Tammy can be, and I'm going to go up to her room right now and make her call him and apologize."

As he stood up, Melody did too. "She won't do it, Brand," she told him in a low voice. "I tried to talk her into it this afternoon but she doesn't have the courage."

"Courage nothing!" he exclaimed impatiently. "She'll call him and apologize at once!"

"You can't force her to do it!"

"Oh, yes, I can, and if I have to spank her I'll do it!" he said grimly.

"No!" Melody's voice was sharp and she moved quickly to stand between him and the door. "You can't do that," she said shakily. "Tammy is fifteen years old! She's a young woman, Brand, not a child anymore! You can't spank her!"

"I can and I will!" he growled at her. "She's my sister and I'll deal with her as I see fit!"

"No," Melody answered hotly, now just as furious as he. "Tammy's in my charge! You said so. You said that was why you married me again! It's obvious you know nothing about teenaged girls, Brand! I promise you, if you storm up there and spank her, you'll lose her regard forever!"

He frowned at her, and for a moment she thought he was going to shove past her anyway. But after a moment he calmed down a bit and said in a calmer voice, "Then

118

what do you suggest? We've got to resolve the situation somehow."

"No, that's just what we can't do," she said appealingly. "Don't you understand, Brand? Tammy's in love with Jim." When he snorted disbelievingly, she rushed on, "Oh, I admit it's puppy love, but the pain is just as real, and, believe me, she is in pain. We simply can't interfere. She's got to be left alone to deal with her own personal relationships. She was hurt and defensive and that's why she lashed out at him like she did. If we just leave them alone, perhaps they'll resolve the problem themselves."

Brand gazed at her unwaveringly for a long time, and then he smiled bitterly. "It seems that the love-life of none of the Traverses can run smoothly, doesn't it?"

Melody lowered her gaze to somewhere midway down his chest. Soft color stole into her cheeks but she refused to be drawn.

"Our love did run smoothly at one time," Brand told her softly. "What happened to us, Melody?"

She shook her head, unable to answer him, and just then the doorbell rang, slicing a sharp knife through the heavy tenseness between them.

"I'll get it," Brand said after a moment, and then he walked out of the room.

The visitor was Lorraine. As Melody followed Brand a minute later, she found the two of them standing in the hallway.

"This is a surprise, Lorraine," Brand said.

Lorraine smiled winsomely. Melody had never seen her looking better. She seemed positively vivacious this evening and her sparkling gray eyes held a hint of blue that matched the dress she wore. Comparing her own to Lorraine's flawless appearance, Melody felt somehow untidy in her neat, simple green dress.

"I brought along some letters for you to sign," Lorraine said to Brand as she held out a sheaf of papers. "You didn't make it back to the office from your meeting this afternoon and I knew you wanted these to go out as soon as possible, so I thought I'd stop by and get your signature and then drop them off in the mail on my way home."

"That's very thoughtful of you," Brand said with a warm smile, "although it's certainly above and beyond the call of duty. I'll be at the office tomorrow morning and they could have waited until then, but thank you anyway. Why don't you come in and join us in a cup of coffee while I sign these?"

"I'd love to," Lorraine answered quickly. Only then did she look beyond Brand and acknowledge Melody's presence with a tiny smile.

Thirty minutes later, Melody set her coffee cup on the lamp table and stood up. Her presence was superfluous and had been all along. Brand and Lorraine were so engrossed in business conversation that she was sure neither of them were even aware she was still in the same room with them.

Brand glanced up in vague surprise as she rose. "You're not leaving us, are you?" He smiled and there was warmth in his eyes as he apologized. "We've been boring you with all this business talk, haven't we? Stay and I promise we'll talk about something else."

Melody was surprised that Brand should bother to encourage her to stay. Surely he would prefer to be alone with Lorraine. He was probably just going through the motions of politeness just for form's sake, she decided with sudden bitterness twisting her lips, and the sooner she removed herself the happier he would be.

"I thought I'd check on Tammy," she answered smoothly, "so if you'll both excuse me?" She forced a smile. "It was nice seeing you again, Lorraine," she added politely, hoping lightning wouldn't strike her dead as she said it.

Lorraine nodded her head graciously and Melody went from the room, overwhelmingly tired and depressed as her mind formed a mental picture of the two people moving close together, entwining their arms around each other now that they had the privacy to do so. She was making it easy for them, she knew, by leaving the room. She was, in effect, giving them a clear field, but she was no watch dog, and she had no intention whatever of playing such a distasteful role.

On Saturday the late afternoon was hot and sultry. Scarcely a hint of breeze stirred the air. The waters below the bluff lay placid and still, the cool blue overlayed with molten gold from the relentless sun above.

Melody leaned back in her chair and closed her eyes briefly, praying that no one would guess how ill she felt. The heat seemed to sap all of her energy and only intensified her dull headache. She was also aware of nausea and now she swallowed hard, willing the sick feeling to pass.

Conversation on the patio swirled around her, but for the moment, it seemed far too much of an effort to attempt to listen, much less take part. There was Brand, Carl, Nicole, and Dale and Marie, who had dropped in unexpectedly. Marie and Nicole seemed to take to one another immediately and were gossiping like two very old friends so that Melody felt safe to rest for a minute or two.

She supposed her ill feeling stemmed from her restless night. She had gone to bed after checking on Tammy, who had fallen asleep on a tear-soaked pillow, but sleep for herself had been impossible. Her mind had continually wandered downstairs, wondering what was happening in the living room. Brand had not come up to bed himself until after two. She knew that because she had glanced at the luminous dial of the bedside clock when she had heard him coming up the stairs. She had pretended to be asleep, of course, but it had been hours before she had dozed off and even then she had slept only fitfully.

Why, she asked herself now, as she had done so many times in the past, is he so determined to hold me as his wife when he loves someone else?

Just now she watched him, without seeming to do so, as he played to perfection the urbane host. He was carrying on an animated conversation with Carl and Dale, appearing to be enjoying himself thoroughly, and she wondered if she would ever really know him, ever really understand him. He was such a complex man . . . a man who could be firm yet forgiving to her erring brother, a man who could be open and friendly with his guests, yet also a man who could blackmail a woman into marrying him, while being both tender and cold to her. He was also a man who led a double life, too, she thought grimly as she remembered last night. No, she decided, she would probably never understand him because Brand would never allow her close enough to him for that.

"Who's staying with your children now?" Marie asked.

Melody came back to the present as she heard Nicole reply, "Our nephew, Jim." She shook her head in a slightly puzzled manner. "I thought he'd want to come with us this afternoon to see Tammy, but he offered to stay with the boys, so we jumped at it. He's so good at handling them. Where is Tammy today, anyway, Melody?"

Melody shrugged carelessly. "Off to a movie with a couple of girl friends," she answered. It was obvious that Nicole knew nothing of the scene between Jim and Tammy, so she kept quiet herself.

"It's just as well that Jim didn't come with us, then," Nicole commented. "He would only have been bored."

A few minutes later, as Marie and Nicole got into a discussion about the latest books, Melody took the opportunity to slip into the kitchen. Before she had left for the day, Juanita had prepared a cold buffet supper for them of sliced meats, salad greens, and fruit compotes. Melody busied herself getting things ready to carry to the patio, glad to have this respite from the heat and the pressure of having to make conversation. When she had everything together, she would go upstairs and find something for this nausea and headache before she returned outdoors.

She pulled a platter of chilled meats from the refrigerator and carried it to the counter. As she did, the kitchen door opened and she looked up to see her brother. Her moment of solitude seemed to be at an end. Hiding her disappointment, she managed a smile of welcome. "Need something?"

"More ice," Dale said. "But I also came to offer help."

"Thanks, but I've just about got everything done. I could use help carrying the trays outside, though."

"Sure," Dale agreed as he came to stand in front of her, "but before we go, tell me what you think about Marie, Sis."

"She seems like a very nice person," Melody answered readily. "I like her."

Dale sighed heavily. "Yeah. So do I. In fact, I love her."

Melody laughed. "Aha! My playboy brother's heart has been snared at last!" she jibed. Then she asked curiously, "And does she feel the same about you?"

Dale shook his dark head and stared glumly at the refrigerator. "I don't know."

The light, teasing smile faded from Melody's face. Something was bothering Dale. "Have you asked her?" she probed gently.

Once more he shook his head. "No."

Melody's hands went to her hips in a gesture of exasperation. "For heaven's sake, Dale, why not?"

Now her brother met her eyes and there was deep unhappiness darkening his. "Surely you understand, Mel," he said at last. He turned abruptly from her and went to stand facing the window. "If I told Marie how I feel about her and found out that she feels the same, I'd ask her to marry me. I just wouldn't be able to stop myself."

Thoroughly perplexed now, Melody went to stand behind him. "And what would be so terrible about that? If you want to marry her, that is?"

Dale whirled around to face her and his eyes were blazing. "Of course I want to marry her!" he exploded.

123

"More than anything in this world. But wives cost money—especially when a family starts to come along—and I can't afford that for years!" His voice was gruff, and before Melody could so much as say a word, he pounded his right fist into the palm of his left hand with sudden violence. "I fouled your life up good and because I did I have no right to look for any happiness myself until I do what I can to straighten things out for you. I told you I was saving every dime to pay Brand back, and I intend to do just that as soon as possible so I can ask him to let you go. How could I possibly ask someone to marry me under such circumstances? It wouldn't be fair to you, Mel!" His voice vibrated with emotion as he added in a softer voice, "You came through for me when I needed you and I'll never forget it."

"That's what relatives are for, Dale," she said shakily with a tremulous smile. "To help each other. And you haven't ruined my life, so don't think it."

"No?" Dale sneered. "Then why do I see you looking so dreadfully unhappy all the time?"

Melody was startled and she began automatically to protest. "That isn't true. I . . ."

"Don't bother denying it," he told her. "I can see it. I'm your brother, remember? I know you and I can see what I've done to you."

She shook her head and lightly touched his arm in appeal. "No, Dale. It's your fault I'm married to Brand again, yes, but if I'm unhappy, it's my own problem, not yours. I assure you Brand doesn't mistreat me."

"I never supposed he did," he said, dismissing the notion entirely, "but because of me you couldn't marry the man you really loved and . . ."

"Rob? No, you mustn't feel guilty about that. I've already discovered that I don't love him. It would have been a terrible mistake if I had married him."

"Then what is making you so unhappy, Mel?" he asked insistently.

She smiled and shook her head. "It's nothing. Don't

124

worry about me. Now, about Marie," she went on quickly, to get off the subject of her own personal life, "if she'll have you, grab her, Dale. She's a fine person and I'd like to have her as a sister-in-law."

"But I just explained . . . " he began.

Melody shook her head vigorously. "We both know that even if by some miracle you could repay Brand every cent tomorrow he still would not let me go. Even if he never prosecuted you, he could ruin you by letting the truth be known, so go ahead with your own life and be happy, Dale. No good purpose can be served by your being miserable. Brand will always have this big stick to hold over me and he knows it, so we might as well face the truth. He will never let me go."

"Quite right," a voice said from the doorway. "I'm glad you understand the situation so perfectly."

There stood Brand, lounging against the door frame, arms crossed over his chest as though he had been there a long time.

"You had no right to eavesdrop on us!" Melody snapped with sudden fury.

Brand's lips stretched into a grim smile. "No? But one can hear quite interesting conversations that way sometimes."

"And never any good about oneself!" she hissed.

"As long as you're here, Brand," Dale said in a tight voice, "and you overheard us, let's have it out, shall we?"

Brand's thick eyebrows rose, he unwound his arms and came further into the room with an easy grace in contrast to the tension of the other two. "Have what out, Dale?" he asked in a lazy drawl.

"I want you to promise that as soon as I have paid you back every cent I owe you that you'll let Melody go free."

"Sorry, pal," Brand said lightly, "but I can't do that. Like the lady just told you, I'll never let her go." Now his gaze flickered across Melody's pale face. "Our guests are waiting for us," he reminded smoothly. "Don't you think we'd better join them?"

125

Chapter Ten

The waves lapped rhythmically against the sides of Gramps's boat, making the only sound to be heard except for the occasional cry of a gull overhead in the cloudless sky. Off in the distance was hazy St. Joseph's Island. Melody's eyes squinted as she scanned the horizon. Although she wore a hat to protect her from the harsh glare of the sun, she had forgotten to bring along her sunglasses.

The boat rocked with a jerky, uneven movement and Melody turned her attention toward her husband. There was a half-smile on his face as he reeled in his line to find a nice-sized trout, the first of the day.

"Congratulations," she said admiringly.

Brand grinned at her as he unhooked the trout and put it on the stringer before tossing it into the water. The sun cast a reddish glint to his black hair and his dark eyes seemed to reflect some of the diamond-brilliant sparkle of the water. "I always said you were my lucky charm," he reminded her.

She smiled at him a bit wistfully. "Too bad it only applies to fishing," she said without thinking.

Brand's smile faded, to be replaced by a quick frown. "Yes," he agreed in a suddenly icy voice, "it is too bad, isn't it?"

Melody chewed her bottom lip. Now why had she said that? she asked herself in frustration. So far this morning, Brand had been agreeable and pleasant, a nice change from his anger yesterday when Dale had attempted to bargain with him for her freedom. Now she had gone and spoiled the peace that had stretched between them.

With a sigh, she reeled in her own line and replaced the bait that some underwater creature had stolen without her even being aware of it. Then, with practiced ease, she cast again. The line sang as it flew out over the water.

They were both silent for a time, but soon Melody squirmed uncomfortably and brushed the back of her hand against her perspiring forehead. She was dismayed to realize the nausea of the day before had suddenly returned. With each swaying motion of the boat, she was feeling worse.

"What's the matter?" Brand asked in a sharp voice. "Sorry you came?"

She glanced at him in surprise. His jaw looked hard and firm and his dark eyes glittered. He had definitely lost whatever good humor he had earlier possessed.

"I'm just hot, that's all," she prevaricated. "And feeling a little cramped. It's been a long time since I've been cooped up in a boat where I can't move." Her stomach churned and she grimaced slightly. She must have caught some virus, she thought miserably, but she had no intentions of admitting to Brand that she felt ill.

An instant later, she was glad she had kept her silence. Stony-faced now, Brand said, "You're not enjoying yourself a bit are you? I can remember when you used to enjoy staying out here all day, but the truth is you just can't stand being alone with me anymore, can you? No doubt you'd enjoy it a lot more if your ex-fiancè were here with you instead."

His words were like a burning match to kindling. Melody had had enough. She had endured more than enough at this man's hands, and now, for him to taunt her while she was feeling so ill, was the limit! He was spoiling for an argument and suddenly so was she!

"Yes!" She answered shrilly. "Yes! Yes! Yes! You're right, of course! I'd *much* rather Rob were here with me! Now are you happy?" She glared at him with fire, sparks flashing in her eyes.

Brand's furrowed brow pushed low over his narrowed eyes. "When you ran away from me," he said in a strange, unnatural voice, "did you run to him?"

Melody turned her head, unable to bear the penetrating intensity of his gaze. The waves that slapped against the boat sent a salty spray across her face but she was totally oblivious to it. "Does it matter?" she countered in a tight voice.

"Hell, yes, it matters!" Brand exploded. "It matters a lot whether my wife was cheating on me behind my back before she deserted me without so much as a word!"

Melody's jaw hardened and her eyes glittered with pure hostility as she swung around to face him. "It's none of your business at all," she told him in a cold, bitter voice, "unless you're ready to reciprocate and confess the hidden affairs you had while we were married!"

His hand shot out across the space between them and he grabbed her wrist. "Just exactly what are you getting at?" he growled from low in his throat.

"Physical violence, Brand?" she jeered as she twisted her arm in an effort to free herself. "All this will get us is landing in the water!" Even as she spoke, the boat lurched sickeningly.

Brand released her, and as the boat settled again he ordered in a dangerously quiet voice, "Explain what you meant. This isn't the first time you've hinted at something and it's time we cleared this thing up, once and for all!"

"I don't have to explain a thing to you!" she snapped angrily as she rubbed her sore wrist. "You're enjoying playing games with your innocent, puzzled air, but it won't work! I'm not the stupid, naïve little girl I once was!"

"You're accusing me of having an affair while we were married?" he asked scornfully. "Let's not be ridiculous, Melody. There's no sense throwing wild and groundless accusations at me just to cover up what you did." He shook his head. "All I know is that my wife left me without a word and I want to know the reason. I *will* know the truth sometime, so you may as well admit it now. Was it because you went to that man you were engaged to? I have a right to know the truth."

"Right!" Melody felt almost hysterical. "You have no

128

rights at all as far as I'm concerned!" she cried. "You may have forced me to marry you again but that doesn't force me to give you any sort of explanation at all. Especially when it is needless. You know as well as I do why I left you, Brand Travers, and until you decide to be open and honest with me, you certainly can't expect me to be open and honest with you! If I could, I'd leave you again this minute and I'd go away so far you could never find me! I hate you, Brand! Do you hear me, I hate you! Is that what you want to live with for the rest of our lives?"

The tirade ended and Melody buried her face in her hands. Her entire body was trembling from the silent sobs that clogged her throat. All was quiet for a full minute and then she could feel movement as Brand shifted around, rocking the boat slightly.

Melody remained with her face covered, as she struggled to get a grip on her emotions and the sick nausea that was again attacking her. She only lifted her head when she heard the motor spring to life. She looked across to see Brand's taut back as he looked out over the water. He was heading them toward shore, she realized with a deep sense of relief.

Tammy and Kathy Elbert, who had come along for the day, had stayed at the elder Traverses', opting against fishing in favor of sunbathing and listening to a blaring radio on the sundeck. Gramps had not gone out on the water with them either because he was suffering from a strained back. Now all three of them met Brand and Melody at the pier, enquiring whether they had caught enough fish for lunch.

It took a supreme effort of will for Melody to get through the remainder of the day. Gram expected them to stay for the Sunday noon meal she so loved to prepare and Melody was forced to spend endless hours smiling and pretending all was well. Her nerves were stretched to the breaking point and she could tell by Brand's rigid posture that he was having a struggle, too.

At least, Melody told herself as she poured tea into ice-filled glasses, the nausea she had suffered earlier had passed. Must have been a twenty-four-hour virus, she decided, and she felt grateful that that misery, at least, no longer plagued her.

Melody stole a sideways peek at Brand. His profile might have been chiseled from stone, so rigid and colorless was it. His entire attention seemed to be on the highway, but she knew that an active brain was working behind that rock-hard exterior. What was he thinking? she wondered. Was he mulling over the scene between them, the hateful words they had hurled at one another?

Her own thoughts swirled in a mist of confusion and anger. She had outright told him that she knew of his affair in the past, yet obstinately he would not admit she was right. Why? How did he hope to conceal what she already knew? True, she had not mentioned Lorraine by name, but there had been no need for that. It was enough to say that she knew.

Yet Brand had called her charges ridiculous, a cover-up for her own actions. He had imputed that she had been cheating on him while they had been married. How laughable! she thought sourly, not in the least amused. And how convenient for him to make such a charge. It was a way of varnishing over his own affair by accusing her of having done the same!

Could it be possible that he actually believed what he said? Right now she hoped he did. If Brand thought she had left him for another man, somehow in a twisted sort of way it was a boost to her own pride. It showed that even while he was being unfaithful to her, he at least acknowledged her own appeal to other men.

What a mess it all was, she thought wearily. And she could see no solution to it at all. She had told Brand she hated him and at this particular moment it happened to be true. She glanced again at his hard profile. He must hate her too, she realized suddenly, because Brand was not the type to forgive a woman for something like infidelity. It might be all right for him, but never his wife! She laughed inwardly with total disillusionment. The good old double standard was still alive and well!

When they arrived home, Brand shut himself away in his study and Melody went upstairs for a bath. She was utterly exhausted, both physically and mentally, and she yearned for nothing so much as an opportunity to be alone for a while.

The hot bath soothed tense muscles, but it did nothing for jangled nerves. After she was dressed in a nightgown and robe, Melody moved restlessly around the bedroom. It was too early to think of sleeping and the truth was that she already knew it would be another one of those nights when the oblivion sleep offered would be long in arriving. Neither a book nor TV offered any appeal at the moment either.

Sighing, she left the room and made her way downstairs. The door to Brand's study was still closed, she was frankly relieved to note, and hurriedly she slipped into the kitchen, where she heated some milk. A few minutes later, carrying the tall mug of milk with her, she let herself out the patio door.

It was a dark night and it suited her mood somehow to sit and listen to the waves licking the shore below. The velvet air, thick with the scent of roses, was cooling against her face, and gradually the peacefulness of the silence relaxed her.

She had been there for more than an hour, reluctant to return indoors where she would inevitably have to face Brand again, when the sliding open of the patio door disturbed her. She glanced up, expecting to see Brand, but instead it was Tammy. For an instant, she remained very still in the dark shadows, hoping the girl would not see her sitting there and would soon go away. She was still overwrought enough not to want conversation with anyone.

The hope was vain. "Melody? Are you out here?" Tammy's voice punctuated the thick night air as she stood, a shadowy figure herself, in the doorway.

Melody chewed her lip in mild aggravation and after a moment forced herself to answer cheerfully, "Yes, Tammy. I'm here."

Tammy came out and closed the door behind her. "What are you doing sitting out here alone in the dark?" she asked.

"Just enjoying the quiet," Melody responded as the girl dropped into a nearby chair.

They both sat in silence for a while, but it was no longer a peaceful silence for Melody. Tammy's presence had shattered that. She sensed that the girl had something on her mind and she waited for her to speak. Even so, it was a shock when it came.

"Are you and Brand going to get another divorce?" Tammy blurted without preliminaries.

Melody's fingers tightened on the arms of the chair and she sucked in a sharp breath. "A divorce! What makes you even ask such a thing?" she gasped.

"Because Brand is upstairs right now moving his clothes out of your bedroom into the guest room," she answered. "What happened, Melody? Have you two had a big fight or something?"

Stunned, Melody could only stare blankly at the younger girl's shadowy features, grateful that the darkness shielded her own face from scrutiny. A strange numbness spread through her, paralyzing both her mind and her limbs.

Brand moving out of their room, and without a word to her! Feeling returned to her body, a rushing torrent of cold, icy cold, anger, far more dreadful and consuming than a hot rage.

How *dare* he humiliate and embarrass her this way . . . allowing Tammy to see him, to be the one to report it to her, his wife! She would never forgive him for this! Never!

But Tammy was still there, waiting for an answer to her question. Melody pulled herself together and was quite proud of the fact that when she spoke it was with calm dignity, giving no hint of the seething turmoil within. "It's a private matter that concerns only Brand and myself, Tammy, and I don't intend to discuss it with you," she said firmly.

"But it *is* my business, too!" Tammy insisted stubbornly. "If you're going to leave, it will affect me as well as you and Brand. It'll mean Brand will send me away to another boarding school again after all and I don't want . . ." Her voice broke as she choked over tears before going on with a rising shrillness, "I knew it was too good to be true! I *knew* this would happen! Why did you have to come back at all? I was just starting to l-love you again, but now I hate you, Melody. I hate you more than anybody or anything in this world!" She jumped to her feet and rushed toward the house.

Melody let her go. There was no possibility of dealing with Tammy while she was in such a state, and besides, under the circumstances there seemed no comfort she could possibly offer, no reasonable explanation to be given.

Tammy's outburst had shaken her. "I hate you!" Words that had been bandied about far too freely this day. It was what she had told Brand that morning, and now Tammy had said the same thing to her. And Brand was moving out of their room.

The peacefulness of the night was shattered, the world suddenly turned upside down. So why did the tide still wash in? Why did the wind still blow? Why did the moon still cling to the sky? It seemed incredible that outwardly everything was still the same and yet nothing was the same.

She stood up, unconsciously squared her shoulders for the ordeal ahead, and with purposeful steps she crossed the patio and went inside the house.

She found Brand in their bedroom, emptying a bureau drawer of neatly folded shirts. He was not aware of her presence because his back was turned to her. She watched him for a moment in swiftly mounting anger and then she closed the door behind her with a thud.

Brand turned and they stared at one another. His face was paler than it had been earlier in the day, and there were harsh lines slashing down his cheeks. His hair was tousled as though he had repeatedly run his fingers through it and just now his eyes were dull and muddy dark pools.

Tension vibrated between them like a tangible entity. Melody knotted and unknotted her fists at her sides and her heart pounded so violently in her breast that she was sure he could hear it all the way across the room.

"So . . . it's true," she said at last in a ragged voice. "Tammy told me you were moving out."

He nodded. "Yes. I think it's best."

"Are you," she asked, almost strangling over the words, "planning to move out of the house?"

"No. Only to the spare bedroom." He turned abruptly and began rummaging through the chest of drawers again.

The action enraged Melody and swiftly she crossed the room to his side. "You can't do this!" she hissed at him in a fierce undertone.

Brand lifted his head and there was a sneer on his face. "No? Just watch me."

"You can't!" she insisted. "You've already gotten Tammy all upset and next it'll be the servants talking and pretty soon everyone else. Well, I won't stand for it, Brand! Do you hear me?" Impulsively, without taking time to think, she lashed out at him and knocked the shirts he held to the floor.

Brand turned on her with the sudden quickness of a snake striking and gripped her arms and began to shake her. "Understand this, Melody," he growled, "I'll do exactly what I want to do and there's nothing you can do to stop me." Roughly, he thrust her away from him and she fell back across the bed. "Stay out of my way," he added.

Dazedly, she sat up on the bed and with a shaking hand pushed her hair away from her face, unaware that her robe had fallen open, revealing heaving breasts above the skimpy, lowcut nightgown she wore. "Why?" she asked dully. "Why are you doing this?"

Brand threw her a black look. "Surely it's obvious after this morning," he answered. Then, curtly, with derision in his voice, he said, "That little trick won't work. Your body holds no allure for me just now, so you may as well cover yourself up decently."

Hot waves of embarrassment and anger stained her face. "I wasn't," she protested as her trembling fingers sought to bring the folds of the robe together across her breasts. "I . . . damn you, I was *not* trying to seduce you!" she sputtered.

He cocked an eyebrow, showing his disbelief. "No?"

"No!" She gave a weary shake of her head. "Look," she said in a tired voice, "wouldn't it be easier just to let me go?"

Violently he slammed his hand against the top of the chest and then he stalked toward her until he stood menacingly over her. "Damn it all, Melody, I've heard just about enough from you on that subject. You are *not* leaving here. Not if you want to save your brother's skin," he added cruelly.

"Why not? It's obvious you don't want me anymore." Bravely she met his eyes without flinching.

He gave a harsh laugh. "You're quite right, I don't. For a while, I thought it just might be possible for us to have a normal marriage in spite of the past, but I was wrong. You made that clear enough this morning. However, the reason I married you still exists and you're staying."

"While you move to another room and start up gossip!"

He turned from her again. "I don't much care about

135

that," he said in a bored tone. He went to the closet and began pulling out slacks and jackets.

Melody struggled to her feet. Blood surged to her face as she glared at him. "Maybe you're not concerned, but I am!" she cried. "You're doing this just to embarrass and humiliate me, aren't you?"

Brand gave her a half-smile. "I hadn't thought about it in just those terms," he said, "but now you mention it, I don't really mind if it does. After all, you rather embarrassed and humiliated me five years ago when you moved out on me!"

"I hate you, Brand!" she gasped furiously. "And I'll never, never forgive you for doing this!"

Brand shrugged disinterestedly. "I can live with that," he said calmly.

"And what about Tammy?" Melody demanded. "This thing has her all upset. She thinks we're getting another divorce."

"She'll soon see she was wrong, won't she?" he said reasonably. "Everything will go on just the same," he told her. "Except that we'll no longer be sharing a room . . . or a bed." He threw a batch of clothes on hangers across his shoulder and then he paused to look at her once more. "You should enjoy sleeping alone again, Melody. It'll leave you free to dream undisturbed about the man you didn't marry. Pleasant dreams."

A moment later he was gone and Melody sank weakly onto the huge, empty bed.

Chapter Eleven

It was late when Melody awoke the next morning. She had suffered a restless night, falling into a deep sleep from sheer exhaustion only after long hours of tossing and turning. She showered and dressed in a pair of white shorts and a cool, printed cotton top and was shocked when she went to stand before the mirror at how pale and drawn she looked. There were violet circles beneath her eyes and the eyes themselves were dull and lifeless.

She had told herself repeatedly that Brand would never hurt her again, and as she stood there some reserve measure of strength and pride reasserted itself. She would *not* allow his actions to upset her! Determinedly, she began applying makeup, soft eye shadow, a cover-up for the circles, a bright, gaily colored lip gloss. Come what may, she would face it with a smile. If there was going to be gossip and speculation about them, so be it, but no one would ever guess from looking at her that she had been deeply crushed.

By the time she went downstairs for breakfast, Brand had already left for the office. Juanita served her bacon and eggs and Melody wondered whether the old woman had heard yet about the household change. But if she had, she kept her peace and Melody was grateful for that.

She had thought she was hungry, but somehow just the smell of food brought on a renewed attack of nausea, and Melody was disgusted with herself for this come-and-go type illness. She only picked at her food as her stomach protested squeamishly and she could not bring herself to touch the coffee. Instead she drank the orange juice, which seemed to help a little.

The morning newspaper lay on the table but she did not bother to pick it up. Her mind was still too dulled from the events of the previous night and she knew she would not assimilate a thing.

She was just about to leave the table when Tammy came in and dropped into a chair opposite her.

"Good morning." Melody forced herself to smile. "Did you sleep late, too?"

Tammy shook her dark head. "No, I've been up for ages." She paused and looked searchingly at Melody. "I had breakfast with Brand."

"Oh." For the life of her, Melody could not think of a thing to say to that.

Tammy picked up the salt shaker and began twisting it

137

between her palms. "He said you're not getting a divorce or anything."

"That's right," Melody answered. Her muscles were taut, her voice stilted.

"Then . . . I don't understand!" Tammy exclaimed. "Why did he move out of your room?"

Melody shook her head. "I told you last night that it's between Brand and me alone. I'm sorry, Tammy, but I don't intend to discuss it with you."

"That's just what Brand said!" Tammy said impatiently. "But what you both don't seem to understand is that I live in this house too!"

Melody smiled in spite of herself. "Yes, you do, but some things are private, even from you. You don't tell me all the secrets you share with your girl friends, now do you?"

Tammy gave her a reluctant grin. "Touché," she said with a little laugh. She replaced the salt shaker on the table and picked up the newspaper. "There are a lot of ads today for back-to-school sales," she said in a suggestive voice.

Melody laughed. "And school being just a month away, the matter is suddenly urgent, huh?" She looked the girl over with a critical eye. "You've lost more weight, Tam," she said with surprise. She supposed she had been so preoccupied lately with her own concerns that she hadn't really noticed. "In fact," she went on slowly, "you're the perfect size now. But your clothes are all too large for you, aren't they? Yes, I think you're right. It's time we got started shopping for school clothes. We'll do it today. Let's make a list first, shall we?"

Fifteen minutes later their heads were close together as they sat on the sofa in the living room. "All right," Melody said as she studied the paper in her hand, "Jeans, shirts, blouses, skirts, a few dresses and . . ." The ringing of the doorbell cut her off. She looked enquiringly at Tammy. "Expecting anyone?"

Tammy shook her head. "Nope." She rose to her feet. "I'll get it."

She went out into the hall and in only moments was back, all color drained from her face as an equally white-faced and solemn Jim Simon trailed behind her.

"Good morning, Jim," Melody said politely as she rose to her feet. "How are you?"

"Fine." He held out a large brown paper bag. "Nicole sent me to bring you some vegetables from her garden."

"How nice!" Melody smiled as she took the bag from him. "Be sure and thank her for me."

"Sure." Jim hung his head and stared at the floor, then mumbled, "Well, I gotta be going."

"Oh, surely not!" Melody exclaimed quickly. "Sit down and visit with Tammy for a few minutes while I take this to the kitchen. Juanita made some peach preserves recently and I'd like to send a couple of jars to Nicole." She ignored the poisonous glare Tammy threw her and hurried from the room.

She hoped it would work, leaving the two of them alone together for a little while. It was the perfect opportunity for Tammy to apologize and she only hoped the girl would take advantage of it.

In the kitchen, Melody placed the bag of vegetables on the counter and then rummaged in the cupboard for the peaches, but though she located them almost at once, she did not return immediately to the living room. She sat down at the table and glanced at her watch. She would give them ten minutes and then she would go back.

The ten minutes ticked by slowly and she was just on the brink of rejoining them when Tammy entered the room, her eyes alight with excitement. "Jim and I made up," she said at once in her forthright manner, "and he wants to know if I can go with him out to the beach for the day. He's got Carl's jeep and we thought we'd ask Kathy and her boy friend to come along too, and . . ."

Melody put on a face of disappointment. "But what

139

about our shopping trip?" she interrupted. "I had thought we'd make a day of it and I was really looking forward to it."

Tammy's face fell. "Oh, that's right." Her shoulders drooped and her smile faded. "I'd forgotten. I'll tell Jim."

Melody giggled as Tammy turned to go. "Silly girl, I was just putting you on. I was hoping you two would get your misunderstanding straightened out. Why do you think I stayed out of the room for so long? Go with Jim and have fun. Just be home before six."

Melody and Juanita had soon packed a picnic basket with food and soft drinks. Tucking Juanita's peach preserves in a corner, Melody sternly admonished the youngsters not to forget to give them to Nicole before leaving for the beach. She was delighted to see Tammy and Jim laughing and joking on the way out as though there had never been any unpleasantness between them.

Melody stood in the drive, waving them off, and just as she was about to turn and go back into the house, Dale arrived unexpectedly.

"What are you doing here this time of morning?" Melody asked in surprise as he stepped out of his car. He looked quite handsome today in a dark business suit and a pale blue dress shirt.

"I had an early morning meeting that only just broke up and now I'm headed for the office," he explained. "I just thought I'd stop by for a minute and tell you my news." His face lit up with a happy grin.

"Marie has been weak enough to accept you," Melody teased.

Dale looked annoyed. "How'd you know?" he growled.

"I can tell by that silly grin you're wearing," she laughed. She moved closer to him and kissed his cheek. "Congratulations, brother. When did you ask her?"

"Last night. That's why I came this morning. I wanted to tell you as soon as possible."

"Have you set a date?"

Dale nodded. "Three weeks from Saturday."

"That soon?"

"Well, neither of us see any sense in a long engagement. Marie's folks live in Ohio and her dad is pretty old and in poor health, so we're going to fly up and be married in her house . . . just a small, private family thing that won't tire him."

"Wonderful! But that means I'd better arrange a shower for Marie as soon as possible. Tell her to call me today so we can discuss the guest list."

"You'd do that for us after what I've put you through?" Dale asked incredulously.

"Don't be silly!" Melody said sharply. "I'm bored with that subject, so drop it!" She gave his shoulder a playful shove in the direction of his car. "I've got far more important things to think about. Now you go away so I can start planning. I've got a thousand things to do! And don't forget to have Marie call me *immediately!*"

Dale laughed. "You're the greatest, Mel!" He enveloped her in a bear hug before he got into his car and with a jaunty wave drove away.

Melody's feet shuffled slowly as she returned to the house. Everybody's romances seemed to be coming up roses, she thought. Everybody's except her own. She stopped herself short. Why in the world should she even *think* of the word "romance" in connection with Brand? True, he had made love to her since they had married again, but that was hardly the same as being "in love." That was simply physical desire—nothing more—and now he no longer wanted her on that intimate basis. That was why he had moved from their room, she reminded herself sternly.

She gave her head an irritable shake. She would not think about that. She would not think about Brand at all. She would concentrate instead on the shower for Marie. That ought to keep her busy and occupied for a while at least, and she was grateful to have something definite to do. It was strange, but when they had been married before she had never seemed to lack for things to do, even with such competent household help as they had. But this time she still felt the outsider and she was reluctant to do some of the things she might have to the house or of rejoining some of the clubs to which she had formerly belonged. All that had been easy enough when she had felt secure in her marriage, but it was different now.

She ate a light lunch and then went into Brand's study and sat down at the desk. She smiled as she picked up a pen and started her list. Earlier she had been working on Tammy's list; now it was a wedding shower. Today seemed to be a day for getting organized.

She sighed and stared unseeingly at a painting on the wall. It was a shame that people could not organize and manage their emotions and relationships with others so easily, but life could not be reduced to simple lists to be followed step by step. Life was an unchartered course over stormy waters with far too many dangerous undercurrents to trap and harm the unwary.

Melody chewed her lip. She was allowing herself to become entirely too introspective. Resolutely, she began writing. She would need invitations, decorations, refreshments, even a few games to play.

Marie telephoned a short time later, profuse with enthusiastic thanks, and the two of them spent a few agreeable minutes discussing the upcoming wedding before they got down to the business of the guest list. They set the date of the shower for one week later, and when they hung up, Melody was satisfied that she had already made a good start. She decided to call Nicole, who was sure to have some excellent ideas for decorations and games, when the telephone rang again.

She scooped it up and gave an absentminded "Hello" as her mind still dwelled on the list in her hand.

"Melody, this is Lorraine White."

Immediately all her attention was on the person at the other end of the line and she tensed automatically. "Yes, Lorraine," she responded coolly. "What can I do for you?"

"I'd like to speak to Brand," came the curt reply.

Melody was surprised. "He isn't here."

"He isn't?" Lorraine's voice sounded as surprised as she felt. "Then where is he?"

"I'm afraid I can't say, Lorraine," Melody answered slowly. "I had supposed he was at the office."

"He hasn't come in at all today," Lorraine stated emphatically. "Nor called."

"That's strange." Melody nibbled thoughtfully on her fingernail. "Perhaps he had some business to attend to elsewhere and forgot to mention it to you," she suggested.

"And you as well?" Lorraine's voice was derisive. "Apparently your marriage leaves a lot to be desired if you don't even know the whereabouts of your own husband."

Melody's knuckles whitened as her fingers pressed tightly around the receiver. "You have an odd concept of marriage," she answered with a calmness she was far from feeling, "if you think a husband and wife should keep tabs on each other's every move. Even in marriage there is a certain amount of freedom."

"Why don't you just give Brand his freedom from you?" Lorraine said spitefully. "He was a happy man until you came back into his life. Now he's often moody and irritable and I know it's all your fault. What good have you ever been for Brand?"

Melody sucked in a sharp breath at the venom in the other woman's voice. "This conversation is pointless, Lorraine. I have work to do as I'm sure you do, too. If Brand should come home early, I'll tell him you called. Good-bye," she ended firmly, before hanging up the receiver.

She stood up and went to the window. As usual Lorraine had managed to upset her and she hated herself for being so weak as to allow it to happen. Lorraine must be very sure of her own relationship with Brand to dare to speak to his wife so bluntly. She seemed to have no fear at all of her words being repeated to him. Melody knotted her hands at her sides. What would happen if she did? Would Brand just laugh it off, tell her his affair with Lorraine was none of her business, or was it possible that if she brought it out into the open he would allow her to leave? Possible yes, but not very probable, she decided at last. Brand's pride would stand in the way of his ever letting her go, no matter how much he might love another woman.

The walls seemed to be closing in on her. Impulsively, she hurried from the room and went upstairs, where she changed out of her shorts into a simple, printed summer dress.

A few minutes later, as she drove away from the house, she felt a sense of release. Somehow it was as though just by the physical act of leaving, she had also left her problems behind. It was an illusion, of course, but it helped all the same.

She had decided to visit Nicole instead of telephoning, and she found her friend delighted to see her. "The boys are napping," she said, "and I'm bored to death. Come in and tell me what's new."

Over glasses of iced tea, Melody told her about the shower for Marie and they spent the next hour and a half happily occupied in the planning of it. It was almost five when Melody glanced at her watch and stood up to leave.

Nicole went with her to the door to see her out. "Looks like the love bug has bitten everyone lately," she said, echoing Melody's earlier thoughts. "First you and Brand got together again, now Dale and Marie, and even Jim and Tammy." She grinned impishly. "I knew they had had a fight of some sort, so that's why I sent him over to your house this morning. I was hoping it would give them a chance to talk and I knew it had worked when he called to tell me she was going to the beach with him."

Melody smiled. "Yes, it worked, although Tammy gave me a look that could kill when I left her in the room alone with him,"

Nicole giggled. "Carl would scold us for matchmaking if

144

he knew." As Melody opened the door to leave, she added, "We've been so busy planning that shower, I don't feel like we got to visit any at all. Why don't you and Brand come over later and spend the evening with us?"

Melody was about to agree when she remembered that Brand had not been to the office earlier in the day. If he were to come home late as well, it would interfere with any plans she might make, and besides, after last night, she could not be sure he would wish to go anywhere at all with her. She shook her head. "I think Brand said something about having a lot of work to catch up on tonight," she fibbed, "so I'd better take a raincheck on it. Thanks anyway."

The afternoon traffic was heavy as she started back home, but Melody did not mind the snail's pace at which she was forced to drive. Home meant Brand, and the new and deeper chasm between them, and she was in no hurry to return to it. And even if he weren't there, the tension of waiting for him to come, the agony of anticipating another scene, would be there in the very walls of the house, surrounding and suffocating her. For a minute she toyed with the idea of going out to dinner and a movie, simply to prolong the inevitable, but then she remembered Tammy. The girl would be returning from her outing with Jim, no doubt full of her day and wanting to talk, and whatever else was wrong with her life, Tammy was the one right thing about it. She certainly did not want to give her any cause for disappointment.

She whipped out of the seemingly endless stream of cars along Ocean Drive into the driveway and pulled around to the back of the house to park the car in the garage. Brand's car was not there, she noted with a sense of relief, as she stepped out of hers.

Opal was in the hall when she entered the house, her purse tucked beneath her arm. "I was just leaving, Mrs. Travers."

"That's fine." Melody smiled. "See you tomorrow."

"Yes, m'am." The maid headed toward the door, then

145

stopped. "Oh, I almost forgot. Miss White called twice and there were a few other calls. I wrote them down on the pad beside the telephone."

Melody nodded. "Thanks, Opal." She had been about to mount the stairs but she paused, then turned and went into the study.

All the calls had been for Brand. Besides Lorraine, there had been three other calls, and Melody recognized the names as business associates of his. She frowned thoughtfully as she replaced the pad next to the telephone. Apparently Brand had not checked in with his office all day—otherwise Lorraine would not have called again and these businessmen must have called his office first, too, before trying the house.

It wasn't like Brand to behave irresponsibly toward his business. In fact, she had never known him to do such a strange thing. A twinge of uneasiness came over her as she pondered where he could possibly be.

Her thoughts were interrupted by the doorbell ringing so she left the study and crossed the hall to the door. When she pulled it open, Lorraine stood there and immediately brushed past her, into the house, without bothering to wait for an invitation. "Has Brand returned yet?" she asked at once as Melody slowly closed the door and turned to face her.

"No, he hasn't. Did he ever call the office?"

"No." Lorraine drummed her fingers against her purse with an agitated gesture. "I thought surely he would be here by this time of day so I brought along some letters that need to be signed. I also have a couple of important messages to give to him."

"Maybe he'll be in shortly," Melody said hopefully. "Would you like to wait for a while?"

Lorraine strode into the living room and then whirled abruptly. Her face and voice were tense. "I think we should call the police."

"The police!" Melody echoed weakly. Her face drained

146

of color and her eyes were wide with sudden fear as she stared at the other woman. "But . . . why?"

Lorraine threw her a scornful look. "Are you entirely stupid?" she snapped impatiently. "Brand is a wealthy man. He could have been kidnapped."

"No!" Melody croaked in a hoarse voice. "No, that's not possible!"

"Of course it is possible," Lorraine insisted. "We can't rule it out. Brand never stays away from the office all day without so much as calling. If he had met with an accident, we'd have heard by now. I tell you, we're wasting time just standing here talking and I'm going to call the police and tell them he is missing!"

Missing! *Brand!* Melody's head spun dizzily at the horrible implication even while her brain rejected it. Nothing could happen to vital, alive Brand! She wouldn't allow it!

In the fraction of an instant between that thought and total oblivion from the excruciating pain that the very possibility brought, she realized the truth that had lain dormant in her heart for so many years, the truth that she had been unconsciously thrusting away for the past few months. She loved Brand. She always had. She could deny it forever, but that would not alter truth one whit. Merciful blackness overcame her.

She was cradled in strong, warm arms when consciousness returned. For a moment she did not open her eyes as she rested in the luxurious, blissful embrace. But harsh voices jolted her peace.

"What happened to her? What did you *do* to her?" Brand's angry voice demanded.

"Me?" Lorraine's voice was derisive. "I didn't do a thing to her. She just passed out. Where have you been all day? I was afraid something dreadful had happened to you."

"I appreciate your concern," Brand answered coldly, "but where I've spent the day is none of your business."

Melody's eyelids fluttered up in her amazement at hearing Brand speak so sharply to Lorraine. At that moment Brand happened to glance down at her, where she lay in his arms. His face was white and haggard, his eyes ice hard, but when he saw that she was conscious, a miraculous transformation thawed his features.

"Melody?" His voice rang out with unmistakable relief and gladness. "Thank goodness! Are you all right?"

"Yes, of course," she murmured. "I'm fine." To prove it, she attempted to sit upright and Brand assisted her, but even then he did not remove his arms from around her.

"Are you sure?" he asked. Anxiety carved ridges across his forehead. "You scared the life out of me. What happened? I've never known you to faint before in your life."

"I was worried about you," she blurted out truthfully. "Nobody seemed to know where you were all day and Lorraine came and said you might . . . might have been kidnapped. She was about to call the police."

"She was, hmm?" He turned his head to look at Lorraine, who stood near the fireplace. "Do you invariably telephone the police with stories of kidnapping every time someone is unreachable for a period of eight hours or so?"

Lorraine flushed a dull red. "Of course not!" she exclaimed with indignation, "but I expected you at the office and . . . "

"Let's get one thing straight, Lorraine." Brand withdrew his arms from around Melody, leaving her with a sudden chilling coldness as he stood up. "You're my secretary, not my keeper, and you'd do well to remember that in the future. I am not accountable to *you* for my movements."

"Brand!" Melody spoke loudly so that both he and Lorraine turned to gaze at her in surprise. She squared her shoulders as she looked at her husband. She did not like Lorraine, but even so she could not allow him to be so unjust to her. "Lorraine was concerned about you, and so was I. You can't blame her for that, surely!"

"I don't need your defense, thank you very much!" Lorraine snapped angrily. She picked up her purse and strode toward the door. A moment later it slammed shut with a resounding bang.

Brand raked his hand through his already mussed hair, sighed deeply, and came back to sink down beside Melody on the sofa. "I suppose I did handle that badly," he admitted, "and you're quite right that I shouldn't blame either of you for being concerned when I seemed to have vanished." He reached out and took one of her hands into his and gazed at it thoughtfully as he continued. "But when I walked in here and saw you in a dead faint on the floor and all she could do was pitch into me, demanding to know where I'd been, I guess I just let my temper get the better of me." He lifted his head and smiled at her. "I'll apologize to her tomorrow at the office. Will that do?"

Melody nodded. She felt choked at the warm expression in his eyes as he regarded her and her skin prickled with acute awareness of his hand touching hers. This was such a different Brand from the hostile, angry man he had been last night, and she wondered at the change in him.

"I want to apologize to you, too," he went on in a low, soft voice. "I never meant to worry anyone, least of all you, Melody. You must believe that. But I had a lot of thinking to do and I needed to be alone." He gave her a wry smile. "I was out on the *Tammy II*."

"All day?" she asked in amazement.

He nodded. His thumb was stroking back and forth with an absent motion across the palm of her hand, sending sensuous vibrations through her entire body, but Brand himself seemed to be unaware of it. "I was thinking about us, the way things are between you and me."

"And?" Melody's breathing stopped as she waited for his answer.

Brand's face went solemn. "And," he said slowly, "I've

come to the conclusion that it's wrong to hold you prisoner in a loveless marriage for a lifetime." He gave a tiny shrug. "I suppose you were right and it was a form of spite, but at the same time I honestly believed we could make a go of it. But it's unfair to both of us. I see that now."

Sickening waves of despair swamped over her like a violent hurricane assaulting the coast. How ironic that just now, when she had discovered she still loved him, Brand should be saying these things! Her mouth was parched and she swallowed painfully. "Brand . . ." she began tentatively.

He cut her off with a shake of his head. "No, let me finish before you say anything," he insisted. "I realize that what I'm about to ask of you is as unfair as all the rest of what's happened, but I'm going to ask it all the same. There's still the problem of Tammy, you see. Already since you've been here she's come far toward being the well-adjusted person she used to be. She admires you and depends on you and it would be a horrible blow to her if you just went away again. So what I'm asking is this—will you please stay for three years for Tammy's sake? Once she graduates from high school, I promise I'll give you your freedom."

"And until then?" she asked huskily, already knowing in her heart what he would say.

"Until then, we'll use separate bedrooms and I will not impose myself on you anymore." His voice grew ragged and abruptly he dropped her hand and stood up, staring woodenly at the wall opposite him. "The least I can do is allow you to be free of my unwanted attentions if you'll agree to do me this one favor." He cleared his throat and glanced down at her. "Well, will you do it? Will you give Tammy three years in return for your freedom?" He gave a bitter smile. "Mind you, you don't have to agree. If you refuse, I'll still let you go. You can walk out that door right now if you want."

Melody looked down at her hands in her lap. They felt clammy and cold and she wondered vaguely if she would ever feel warm again. "I'll stay," she answered at last. "For Tammy's sake." Even as she said it, she knew she was condemning herself to three years of living hell.

Chapter Twelve

Even through the closed bedroom windows upstairs, the shouts and laughter penetrated. Melody crossed the room and opened the medicine cabinet in the bathroom, scarcely aware of the noise outside. It seemed she was always swallowing tablets to relieve her queasy stomach these days. It was probably an ulcer, she had decided, but since the symptoms never lasted very long at a time she had done nothing toward consulting a doctor about it. She knew if it continued much longer, she would be forced to have a checkup.

She went back into the bedroom and paused before the dresser to brush her hair. She seemed to have lost a bit of weight lately, too, she thought as she critically studied her reflection. But then, she had so little appetite these days. She raised her hand to smooth back her hair from her forehead and as she did so, she saw Brand's face in the mirror. He was standing in the open doorway, watching her.

"Hello. I didn't realize you had come home," she said as she turned toward him.

Brand smiled. "I had a rough day so I decided to get away a little early. What's going on out back?"

Melody shrugged her slender shoulders. "The usual gang of teenagers," she answered. "Tammy invited about a dozen boys and girls over for swimming and a weiner roast and later, when the boys go home, the girls will have a slumber party."

Brand grimaced. "At least when Tam was so sullen and

awful, we did have peace and quiet around here. Nowadays I feel like we're running a twenty-four-hours-a-day recreation center."

Melody grinned in sympathy. "Not to mention a free restaurant. I feel like I'm shopping for an army every time I go to the supermarket."

Brand nodded. "It seems we succeeded too well in our aim where Tam's concerned, doesn't it?"

Melody nodded and then, the subject of Tammy exhausted, a stilted silence fell between them. Melody twisted the handle of her hairbrush with an awkward, nervous gesture while Brand loosened his tie.

"How was your day?" he asked after a moment.

"Fine," she answered quickly. "Just fine. I went with Nicole to her ceramics class. I'm thinking of taking it up myself. What do you think?"

"I think it's a good idea if it's what you want," he said readily. "Well, I guess I'll go change my clothes."

"I'm about to go back downstairs," she told him. "I'll fix you a drink if you want."

"That would be nice. Thank you." Brand moved from the doorway and went across the hall and into the bedroom he was using.

Melody turned slowly and replaced the hairbrush on the dresser before leaving the room. It had been like this for the past two weeks, this formal politeness between Brand and herself. Ever since the day he had offered her her freedom, he had been scrupulously attentive to her comfort and pleasure, taking her out to dinner one night, to a party another, and so on, but for her part it was all thoroughly exhausting. Now they found difficulty in carrying on a sustained conversation for any length of time. There was no longer any need to argue, and the intimacy between them had gone, leaving them both as courteous strangers who merely happened to share the same house.

On her part there was a further reticence in their new

152

relationship. Whenever they were alone together, she had held herself in a tight rein, fearing that if she let down her guard for so much as a single instant, Brand might somehow guess her secret. And, above all, she did not want him to know how she felt. She knew she could not bear it if he should ever learn that she still loved him. She could not bear his pity, his continued rejection of her, if he knew.

Even so, in some ways she had been happier the past two weeks than she had been in a long time. Brand could not be faulted in even the smallest degree in his consideration of her; also, she had been agreeably busy every day. The shower for Marie had been a wonderful success and Brand had even thrown a bachelor's party at a club the same evening for Dale. She and Tammy enjoyed their forays for school clothes and it had been a real pleasure for the both of them. Tammy had lost all the weight she needed to, and now she was slender and glowingly beautiful and their only problem had been in deciding what to buy among so many lovely clothes.

As she reached the bottom of the stairs, the din of laughter from the patio was almost deafening. Melody smiled to herself. Brand was right. They had certainly succeeded with Tammy. She had completely lost her old sour disposition now that she realized it had been her own attitude that had kept others at arm's length.

She prepared a Scotch and water for Brand, a lemonade for herself, and carried them into the living room, where the exuberant noise from behind the house was reduced to a dull roar.

She placed both drinks on a table and sat down on the sofa just as Brand entered. He had changed from his business suit into a pair of dark casual slacks and a white leisure suit. His skin was bronzed against the shirt and Melody was struck with an aching awareness of his strongly hewn, masculine good looks. She had an overwhelming desire to fling herself into those powerful arms, to sink into the warmth of his embrace, to drown in the liquid tenderness that had been in his eyes in the past. The sensation was so intense that she actually had to lace her fingers tightly in her lap and will herself to remain still.

Brand seemed oblivious of the storm that raged within her as he came to sit on the opposite end of the sofa, leaving a wide space between them. Calmly he picked up his drink and, after taking a sip of it, began making idle conversation about Dale.

"He's absolutely hopeless," he told her. "Can't keep his mind on a thing." He grinned wryly. "That's what love can do to a man. It can completely destroy his ability to think or act rationally."

"I can't believe it ever affected you that way," she said, and was dismayed at the forlorn little catch in her throat.

"Oh, yes." Suddenly Brand's face went taut and his words were bitter. "I made as big a fool of myself as the next man."

He was thinking of Lorraine, she supposed, and of the fact that he had allowed a desire for revenge to stop him from marrying her. Melody's shoulders drooped a bit and she gazed down at her hands as she blinked back the sudden tears that stung her eyes.

There was a long, thoughtful silence after his statement, but then Brand stirred, as though to shake off black memories, and his voice was light as he said, "Oh, well, I'm sure Dale will come to his senses and revert back to normal once the honeymoon is over. Which reminds me, I've got a surprise for you."

"For me?" She lifted her head and her eyes were wide as she looked at him.

Brand was smiling. "I thought, if you'd like, you and I might just take a short trip to Ohio this weekend."

Melody's eyes lit up. "We're going to the wedding?" she gasped with delight.

Brand laughed and said teasingly, "Well, it would be a shame to waste the two airline tickets I bought today."

She clasped her hands together and smiled. "Brand, thank you! Oh, I did hate the thought of missing my own brother's wedding." She stopped short and asked suddenly, "But what about Tammy?"

He shrugged. "I'm sure Gram and Gramps would be happy to keep her for the weekend, or maybe she could stay with one of her friends."

They left on Friday and Dale and Marie, who had gone ahead two days earlier, met them at the airport in Cleveland and drove them the fifty miles to the small town where Marie's parents lived. "You're to stay at the house," Marie informed them on the drive. "We have plenty of room and Mom and Dad insist."

"I made reservations at a motel," Brand said. "The same one Dale is staying in, I believe."

"That's right, but I already cancelled it for you," Dale said helpfully. "Marie's folks are great and you'll enjoy staying with them, and that way," he chuckled, "Melody won't miss out on any of the activity."

Melody forced a smile to her lips. Since discovering they were coming, both Dale and Marie had asked her and Brand to be their attendants at the wedding and Melody had been pleased to be asked, but actually staying in the house was another matter. It meant, she realized with a sinking sensation, that she and Brand would be having to share a room once again.

Marie's parents lived in a large, shabbily comfortable old house on a quiet, tree-shaded street. Both Mr. and Mrs. Ellis warmly welcomed them, where they found a hot meal awaiting them.

After the meal, both Mrs. Ellis and Marie refused Melody's help with cleaning the kitchen, so she went to the bedroom she and Brand had been assigned and began unpacking.

"I'm sorry," Brand said quietly as he came into the room and closed the door. "But when I planned the trip, I didn't count on this happening." He waved a hand toward the huge double bed which stood prominently in the center of the room.

"I know," she said in a strained voice. "It doesn't matter." She turned quickly back to the opened suitcase in an effort to avoid his eyes.

He crossed the floor to stand beside her and he reached out his hand and gently turned her face toward him. His eyes were dark and searching. "It's only for two nights," he said slowly. "Can you bear to have me sharing your room that long, Melody? If not, just say the word and I'll insist on going to the motel anyway."

She shook her head in a slight movement. "No," she said hoarsely. "It . . . it would be too embarrassing for both of us and . . . and anyway . . ." She paused, then went on swiftly, "I can put up with it for two nights if you can."

Brand smiled but the smile did not reach his eyes. "Good girl," he said approvingly. Then, in a different voice, he added, "I'll help you to unpack."

The wedding went off the next day without a hitch and by nightfall the house was quiet again at last after an exciting and eventful day. Marie had been a lovely bride and Dale a handsome groom, Melody thought proudly. The newlyweds had left for a short honeymoon trip and would be returning to Texas in a week's time. The Ellises seemed touchingly glad to have Brand and Melody as guests again that night now that their only child was married and gone, since they knew that it would be many long months before she would be able to return home for another visit. Melody did her best to be cheerful company, and so did Brand, as he listened with infinite patience to Mr. Ellis's talk about the hardware business, from which he was retired.

At ten o'clock, Melody was relieved when their hosts declared their intention of going to bed. She felt unaccountably drained herself, though she could not understand why. True, it had been a busy day, but not exhaustingly so. She could only suppose it was because she felt so acutely aware of the difference between her brother's marriage and her own.

In the bedroom she undressed, deciding that, though she had bathed that morning, she would take another hot bath with the hopes that it would relax tired muscles. She threw her pale green dress across a chair and added to it slip, bra, and panty hose.

Her bare skin had a rosy glow cast by the lamplight and she reached out toward the back of the chair to pick up her robe when the bedroom door opened. With a jerky movement, she turned. Brand came striding into the room, obviously unaware that she was there, because he halted abruptly and appeared as startled as she was.

For a long moment, they both seemed to be suspended in time as they stared at one another in frozen silence. Melody was mesmerized by the expression of frank desire in his eyes, and she could not have moved or spoken had she tried.

Brand uttered an inarticulate sound and then he had eliminated the space between them. Roughly, almost greedily, he pulled her into his arms, crushing her warm, soft body against the lean hardness of his. With a gentle moan, his lips claimed hers, and with sure instinct her arms moved up and around his neck.

Melody became lost to everything as her senses took control. Her body was throbbingly alive to his touch, to the exquisite emotions that warmed her blood as his hands stroked her bare skin. The masculine scent of him swelled the wild, aching desires within her and she pressed herself closer, closer to him.

She wasn't in the least prepared for what happened next. One instant Brand's lips were bruising hers with hungry passion; the next, with cruel suddenness that snatched her breath away, he shoved her so forcefully that she stumbled and fell back across the bed.

She attempted to focus her eyes that were still bemused

with sensuous desire and her reddened, swollen lips quivered. "What . . . what . . .?" She could not go on as she gazed helplessly at his towering, rigid form, which loomed above her.

With a violent gesture, Brand snatched up her robe and flung it at her. "Cover yourself," he grated menacingly.

Awkwardly, she struggled to sit up, pulling the robe across the front of her body as she did so, but her gaze never left his face. "I . . . I don't understand . . ." she stammered.

"Don't you?" Brand's mouth twisted into an ugly sneer. "I certainly do. Once again you're out to make a fool of me," his voice grated harshly. "You've told me repeatedly how much you hate me, how much you love another man, yet when I moved out of your room and your bed, it hurt your pride so you decided to take advantage of the situation here while we're forced to share a room, didn't you?"

Melody cringed beneath the angry onslaught of words. "You . . . you think I planned this just now?" she asked in disbelief.

Brand gave a short laugh. "I *know* you did!" he responded. "It's not enough that you walked out on me once, leaving *my* pride in shreds, but now you'd do it again! You won't be happy until you see me on my knees, groveling at your feet, will you? But that, my dear *wife*, will never happen!" In two long strides, his legs had carried him to the door and he went out, leaving Melody to stare at the closed door in a state of shock and bewilderment and with a pain such as she had never known.

Brand did not return to the room that night and it was only toward dawn when Melody at last fell into an uneasy, nightmare-tortured sleep.

It was hard the next morning, struggling to appear normal and pleasant as the Ellises drove them to Cleveland to catch their plane. It was harder still to sit beside Brand as the plane carried them south. Not once today had he spoken to her unless it was absolutely necessary and now he ignored her as though she did not even exist.

He thought that she had planned a seduction scene last night, all for the purpose of bringing him to heel. She could not believe he could think so dreadfully of her that she would actually welcome his lovemaking in order to hurt him by it. Melody gazed out the window at a layer of filmy clouds as utter hopelessness clouded her own heart.

She was glad when they reached home at last, where she could go to the room she had once shared with Brand and could be alone. Now that room represented the only safe haven she possessed, because there, she knew with absolute certainty, he would never again seek her out.

Two days later she gave up all pretense to herself about the nausea she had been experiencing the past few weeks. She called Carl Simon's office and made an appointment to see him for the following day when she knew she would be free from the prying questions of others, it being both Juanita's and Opal's day off. Also Tammy would be out of the way, going on an overnight trip with Kathy Elbert and her parents to visit the Brownsville zoo and then on to do some shopping across the Mexican border in the town of Matamoros.

The examination did not take long and once she was again dressed in her white pleated skirt and simple gold blouse, Carl led her into his private office, where he confirmed the suspicion she had until now been thrusting to the back recesses of her mind.

"I'd say you're about two months pregnant, Melody," he told her. "Congratulations!"

Melody managed a wan smile. "Thanks, Carl."

"Does Brand know?" he asked.

She shook her head. "No, I wanted to be sure first," she said slowly.

"We'll have a great celebration," Carl suggested. "Tell you what, Nicole and I will take you both out to dinner this weekend."

She shook her head once more and then gazed earnestly at him from across the desk. "No. If you don't mind, Carl, would you please not say anything to Brand . . . or Nicole either? I . . . I'm not sure if I'm ready to tell him yet."

Carl frowned. "But why not?" He was clearly puzzled. "He'll be delighted. You know that, surely?"

"Yes," she said, hoping the doubt she felt didn't show. "But, well, I'd like to keep it my own secret . . . just for a little while. Just until I get used to it myself."

Carl laughed and nodded his head indulgently. "A pregnant lady's prerogative, of course, the same as wanting pickles or other strange things to eat in the middle of the night. Naturally I won't say a word to anybody, Melody," he assured her. "It's your news to tell, after all, not mine."

Melody stood up to leave. "Thanks, Carl."

"Just a moment before you go," he said. He was scribbling on a prescription pad and now he held the piece of paper out to her. "This is for some high-powered vitamins. You're in excellent health now, but these will help to keep you that way. As for the nausea, it usually disappears along about the third month. Now, I'll want you back in here for a check-up one month from today."

Melody left the office and stepped outside into the hot, blazing sunshine and moved toward the car as though she were in a daze. When she reached it, she unlocked the door and slid inside, but she did not immediately turn the ignition key.

I'm carrying Brand's child, she told herself. A bewildering sensation of both gladness and sadness fought for dominance. Deep within she knew she was glad, that it could not really be otherwise. She glanced down at her still-flat abdomen and felt a surge of great tenderness rush over her. She loved Brand and now she was carrying his baby inside her. Wonder and delight at the sheer miracle of it filled her heart.

But how would the news affect Brand? She dreaded even the idea of having to tell him. He hated her so now.

160

Would he be able to love their child, or would he perhaps believe she had deliberately allowed this to happen so that she might have a permanent hold over him? She frowned. It was difficult to guess what his reaction would be. When they had married the first time, Brand had often expressed his desire for children, but now? It was possible that he might resent having to support a child by a wife he no longer loved. She shook her head in sorrow and lightly touched her hand to her midsection. Poor baby, she thought. Poor, innocent little baby, to have been conceived by revenge and born into a life where its father hated its mother. What an unfair beginning!

When she arrived back home, she was doubly glad to have a silent, empty house to herself. She was slightly tired, but more than rest, she needed time to think, time to absorb this enormously important change that was now affecting her body, that would soon affect her whole life as well.

She dropped her handbag onto a hall table and wandered aimlessly into the living room. If only, she was thinking, her marriage was a normal one, what a celebration she would plan when she gave such wonderful news to her husband! What pure joy she would be experiencing! Instead, she was terrified to tell Brand the truth.

The doorbell rang, jolting her out of her troubled thoughts. She was annoyed as she went toward the door. She was in no mood for company, and if it should be Nicole it would be hours before she could again be alone.

It wasn't Nicole. It was Rob Willis.

"Well," he spoke after a long moment of silence as she stood staring at him as though he were a ghost, "aren't you even going to say hello, Melody?"

Slowly recovering from the shock of seeing him, she nodded vaguely. "Hello, Rob. What are you doing here?"

He gave a tiny smile and the skin crinkled at the corners of his hazel eyes. "I came to see you, of course," he answered. "Aren't you even going to invite me in?"

"Of . . . of course." She pulled the door fully open so

that he could enter and led him into the living room, where they confronted one another as they stood a few feet apart.

"You're more beautiful than I remembered," Rob said softly after a moment.

"Thank you," she said politely. "You . . . you're looking well yourself, Rob. But you never answered my question. What are you doing here?"

He shrugged his shoulders. "I decided to take a few days off from work and come down here to see you. To see how you're doing. I still can't believe you left me Melody—that this marriage of yours is on the up and up. It happened so fast and we were engaged." His voice held an accusing note.

"I'm sorry," she said apologetically as she gazed down at her sandaled feet. "I'll admit it did happen quickly, my remarriage to Brand, but . . ."

"Are you happy?" Rob asked insistently. "I guess that's what I came here to discover. Are you happy this time, Melody? Because if you're not, I want you to know I still love you, that I'm still waiting for you to come back to me if it doesn't work out for you."

She lifted her head at last. "Don't do that, Rob," she told him earnestly. "Wait, I mean. It wouldn't do any good."

He grimaced at that. "Then you are happy? You're really in love with your husband?" His eyes were very penetrating as he studied her face.

"Yes." Her voice was a mere whisper as she acknowledged it. "Yes, I do love Brand. I wouldn't have married him again otherwise," she added for good measure, "so you can see it's no use for you to go on hoping for something that won't ever happen." She felt sorry for Rob and for the obvious pain in his eyes; she knew all about the pain of loving someone who didn't return that love. But it would only hurt him worse in the long run if she was not able to convince him that it was over between them for good, and she was determined to make it crystal clear so

162

that he would leave without carrying any unfounded hopes.

Apparently he read the truth and sincerity in her eyes and words, because he said after a moment, "I suppose I realized it all along, but I had to try. I had to find out the real truth." He attempted to smile at her and his hand went out and clasped both of hers. "I hope you'll always be happy, Melody."

"Thank you, Rob," she added huskily as tears stung her eyes. "You're a . . . you're a grand person and you deserve someone better than me . . . someone who can love you wholeheartedly and without reservation." She gave him a watery smile. "I think you'll find her."

His hands squeezed hers. "I suppose there's nothing more to say between us, then?" he asked.

"No," she admitted. "I suppose there isn't."

"Then, good-bye, Melody." Gently, Rob pulled her into his arms and when he bent his head to kiss her one last time, she did not resist.

An instant later, she was wrenched from his arms by an explosive voice. "Just what in hell is going on here?"

Brand, with dreadful black fury darkening his face, stood near the door glaring at them. Every line of his body was taut with such devastating anger as Melody had never seen, and she swayed slightly from the force of it.

Chapter Thirteen

Although Rob dropped his arms from around her, he did not move away. It was as though he were attempting to shield Melody with his body from the wrath of the man across the room.

His chin jutted out almost aggressively as he faced Brand. "You must be Melody's husband," he said, "and I'd like to explain to you what you just saw."

Brand took a menacing step forward. "There's no need for an explanation," he grated harshly. "I can see for myself." He jerked a thumb toward the door. "Get out of my house!" he ordered.

"Brand, listen . . ." Melody began urgently.

He turned his burning gaze upon her and she flinched beneath it. "Shut up!" he rasped. "I'll deal with you later." He glared once again at Rob. "Are you going or do I have to throw you out?"

"Listen, man, there's no need for violence here. I was just about to leave anyway." Now Rob looked back at Melody. "If you ever need me," he said gently, "you know where to find me."

Melody nodded but she scarcely even heard him. Her entire body was attuned to Brand and his terrible, threatening anger.

Rob moved toward the door but as he drew level with Brand, he halted. "I love Melody," he said simply, "and if I ever hear of you hurting her in any way, you're going to have to answer to me."

Brand's mouth was grim. "You're threatening me in my own home?" he snarled.

Rob nodded. "Yes, because somehow I don't believe you're right for her. If you had been, your marriage would never have broken up the first time." He turned once more to glance back at Melody. "Remember what I told you," he said. Then he went swiftly from the room.

The silence that remained behind after he left was as dense and frightening as a morning fog obscuring the harbor bridge. Melody's throat constricted painfully beneath Brand's antagonistic gaze.

"That was Wallis, of course," he stated at last. "The man you were engaged to?"

"Yes." Her voice came thin and wispy.

His jaw hardened. "I knew it must be, what with the tender love scene being enacted."

Melody licked her lips. "You don't understand," she told him. "It . . . it wasn't like you think."

"Wasn't it?" His dark eyes raked over her with scornful

164

disbelief. "God, I thought I knew you better!" he exclaimed. "I thought you had more decency than to ever invite him *here!* You're shameless and disgusting and I can't bear the sight of you anymore!" He turned his back to her and the muscles across his shoulders and back were rock hard.

"If you'd only let me explain," she pleaded. "Brand, what you say isn't true!"

He whirled to glare at her. "Don't add lies on top of the heap!" he growled. He sucked in a deep breath and then, quite calmly, said, "I'm releasing you from our deal, Melody. I'd like for you to leave as soon as possible . . . preferably tonight. Go back to Dallas with Wallis."

All color drained from her face and her body went limp so that she actually had to brace herself against the back of a chair to keep from falling. "You . . . you can't mean that!" Melody declared in a whisper.

"I mean it, all right," he told her, still in that deadly calm voice devoid of all emotion that was somehow much worse than the anger and violence that had coated it earlier. "You can take the car if you like, and all the money in your checking account. If you need more I'll see that you have it. You can file for divorce and I'll pay all the expenses and we'll call it quits for good."

"What about Tammy?" she asked numbly.

Brand sliced the air with his hand. "Don't worry about her," he said in a freezing voice. "We both managed when you left us the first time and we'll manage again. I'll probably try to hire some nice, mature older woman to be her chaperone so that she can live at home. I'm sure Lorraine will be able to find someone suitable. The main thing right now is that I want you gone. When I leave this room, I never want to see you again, Melody."

Pride stiffened her. His words were like a razor cutting sharply into her heart, but she would not allow him to see that. Now her own chin jutted out and she squared her shoulders. "All right," she agreed unemotionally. "I'll be gone today if that's what you want. I'll take only what I need for the moment and you can send on the remainder of my things later."

Brand nodded. "Fine."

"One more thing, though," she said determinedly. "What about Dale?"

His lips twisted into a bitter smile. "Dale is still your only concern, isn't he? You came back to me only on his account, but you couldn't stick to the bargain you made." He laughed harshly. "You don't need to worry about him, I assure you. Right now I have far more respect for your brother than I do for you. Dale is truly sorry for what he did and he's been working hard to make up for it. And now that he is married, I'm confident he'll stick to the straight and narrow. Which is more than can be said for you!" He shrugged. "I'm not going to prosecute Dale, not ever, so you need not let that concern you."

"Thank you," she said through stiff lips. "Then, if there's nothing else, I'll go up and start packing."

"That's a good idea." He glanced down at his watch. "I've a business appointment in half an hour. I'll just pick up the papers from my study that I had stopped in to get and then I'll leave. You can take your time packing. I won't be home until late tonight."

"I'll be out of the way well before then," Melody promised.

Brand gave her a casual nod and walked toward the door just as though nothing at all momentous had occurred between them.

Melody stood rigid for another moment, and when she was certain he was in the study, her body came alive at last and she made a dash for the stairs.

But as soon as she was inside the privacy of the bedroom, her body went limp again and she sank to the edge of the bed. In a moment she would have to find the strength to get up and begin packing, but for now she knew that task was quite beyond her.

She looked down at her hands and noticed with a

166

strange detachment that they were trembling. She clenched her fists in an effort to still them and happened to notice her wedding rings. No need for them anymore, she told herself as she slipped them off her finger and placed them carefully on the bedside table.

For a long time she made no effort to move. It was as though every ounce of energy had been drained from her, leaving her lifeless, without aim or intent. Even her mind seemed blank. She merely sat there, quiet, her eyes glazing at nothing, her brain unable to function. She was too numb even to shed so much as a single tear.

When she did stir at last, she noted with a jolt of surprise that it was nearing four o'clock. She had returned from Carl's office about a quarter of three and a lifetime seemed to have passed since then. But now the clock was moving ruthlessly onward and she still must pack and find someplace to stay the night.

It all seemed so much to do, and yet she had no choice. Brand had made it abundantly clear that he expected her to be gone before he returned home tonight.

Listlessly, she rose to her feet and went to the closet. She flung the door open wide and pulled out a suitcase. Then her gaze flitted around the room. Where should she start? she asked herself. What should she take?

It did not seem to matter, and after a moment's confused hesitation, she began lifting one thing from this drawer, another from a different drawer, a hanger from the closet. Totally disoriented, she was not even aware of packing an evening dress for which she probably would not have the slightest use and overlooking completely a favorite and practical street dress. She packed panties but no bras, a slip but no nightgown, her portable blow dryer but no hairbrush.

In the middle of all this, she thought suddenly of Tammy and she stopped what she was doing to go downstairs for writing paper and pen. She had no hesitation about entering Brand's study because she knew he would long since have left the house.

The letter was difficult to write, both because of its contents and because of the confused state of her mind. But at last she wrote, and though it left her feeling dissatisfied, it was the best she could do. In the letter she explained that though she was leaving again, this time it had not been her choice, that she loved Tammy very much and that she hoped she would be able to forgive her. Then she folded it and slipped it inside an envelope. She sealed it and scrawled Tammy's name on the outside.

With the letter in her hand, she went out into the hall, about to go upstairs and place it on Tammy's dresser, when the doorbell rang once more.

Melody chewed her lip as she hesitated over whether to answer the door or not. Maybe if she simply remained silent, whoever it was would just go away again. But even as she thought it, the bell rang again, loud and insistent.

She paused long enough to drop the letter onto the hall table and then she made her way to the door. Gram Travers stood there, looking smart and lovely in a beige two-piece suit.

"Gram! What a surprise!" Melody exclaimed. "Come in. Did . . . did Brand know you were coming here today?"

"No," Gram answered as she stepped into the hall. "George had an appointment with the doctor for his regular checkup, so I came along for the ride."

Melody had been about to close the door but now she peered outside. "Where is he? Did he come here with you?"

"No," Gram said again. "He wanted to go visit an old friend while we were here so I told him to drop me off here. My dear," she added in a persuasive voice, "I'm dying of thirst."

Melody managed a quick smile. "I'll get you a glass of tea . . . or would you rather coffee?"

"Tea would be fine," Gram answered as she went into the living room.

Melody went to the kitchen, wishing Gram had not

168

come today of all days. She was sharply aware of the passage of time and of the packing that still remained to be done upstairs. Also, in her present mental condition, she was not sure she was equal to the task of carrying on a lot of small talk and pretending nothing was wrong.

But she had no choice but to try. She picked up the two glasses of iced tea and carried them through to the living room, where Gram was already comfortably installed in an easy chair.

For a few minutes they talked about predictable subjects—Tammy, clothes, the storm that was forming down around the Bahamas which they hoped would not develop into something that might affect the Texas coast. In truth, though, Melody scarcely gave the storm a passing thought. She was too busy battling the storm in her own life.

Conversation suddenly lagged and Melody stared intently at the glass in her hand as she sought for some safe topic with which to end the awkward, little silence.

But it was Gram who did that. "Enough of this trivia, Melody," she said in a firm manner. "There's something wrong and I want to know what it is."

Melody was startled at Gram's perception and her eyes grew wary. "Wh-what could be wrong?" she countered as she attempted a smile.

"You tell me," Gram insisted. "Apart from the fact that you're pregnant, that is."

Melody stiffened and stared at her in amazement, too surprised even to prevaricate. "How did you know?" she gasped.

Gram laughed and took a sip of her tea. "I'm a witch." She cocked her head to the side and studied Melody with bold frankness. "Actually, it was just a shrewd guess. You simply look different, somehow. Maybe it's your eyes. But," she went on critically, "your condition doesn't appear to be making you wildly happy. In fact, you look downright miserable to me. What is it, child?"

The kindness in her voice and the gentle expression in

169

her eyes shattered Melody's defenses, and all at once the words seemed to tumble out over each other as she told Gram everything, holding nothing back. There was no reason not to be completely honest now. Brand had wanted his grandparents to think they had married again because they loved each other and that their marriage was normal in every way, but the time for pretense was over. They would have known soon enough in any case that she and Brand were separated again.

Gram heard her out in silence, her regal face serene as she leaned back against the cushioned chair. Just her very bearing somehow had a calming influence on Melody, and as the story drew to an end her words came slower, her tone more controlled.

"That's quite a tale," Gram said thoughtfully when the story came to an end at last. "A marriage based on such a foundation as revenge, blackmail, and fear would be bound to fail. But there's one thing you neglected to tell me, Melody."

"What's that?" Melody frowned in an effort to think of what she might have forgotten.

"Are you in love with my grandson, child? Despite all that's happened between you?" Gram's eyes were piercing and sharp as she scrutinized Melody's face.

Long eyelashes swept down to shield Melody's eyes. She wanted to lie but her lips suddenly quivered and the truth came out. "Yes," she whispered brokenly. "Yes, I love him, Gram, but it won't do any good because he hates me."

"Hmm," Gram mumbled, "and I suppose you haven't told him how you feel?"

Melody's lashes flew up. "Of course not!" she exclaimed. "I . . . I can't possibly tell him!" She paled at the thought.

"And have you told him about the baby?" Gram's voice was stern now.

"I couldn't." Melody's hands were trembling again and she gripped the iced-tea glass with both of them in an

170

effort to still them. "I . . . I had only just found out for sure today and then he found . . . found Rob here and . . . and . . ." Her voice faded.

"You realize he must be told?" Gram asked. "It's his child, too, and he has a right to know."

"No!" Melody cried out. "No! And you must swear you won't tell him either, Gram! Brand doesn't return my love—I've explained all that to you. So I can't tell him about the baby! He'd be bound to think I was trying to hang on to him by unfair means!"

Gram gave an inelegant snort. "I can't for the life of me understand how that could possibly be misconstrued as unfair. After all, you *are* his wife and it *is* his child you're carrying!"

Melody raised agonized eyes to her face. "Please, Gram!" she insisted. "Promise you won't tell him!"

"Then tell me this, Melody. Just where are you planning to go when you leave here?"

Melody made a vague gesture with her hand. "I . . . I don't know. It doesn't matter."

"So, you'd just completely vanish from our lives again, and this time with my unborn great-grandchild?" Gram snapped with the first hint of anger all afternoon. "No, child, I won't allow that!" As Melody opened her mouth to speak, Gram held up a hand to silence her. "Leave Brand if you must, but the price of my silence about the baby is for you to come stay with us." She smiled, dispelling the harshness of her earlier words. "At least for a while, until you've had time to think things through and you are able to make a rational decision, which you're in no condition to do at the moment." She rose gracefully to her feet and held out a hand toward Melody. "Come on, my dear, and I'll help you pack."

No one, Melody decided the following afternoon as she sat on the sundeck alone, could have been kinder than Gram and Gramps. They were both understanding and considerate and were doing their best to make her at home with them, as though she were a beloved granddaughter in reality. So why, she asked herself crossly, did she feel this constant urge to cry?

Brand was not worth tears, she told herself. He had accused and condemned her without a hearing. He had made up his mind to get rid of her from that night at Marie's parents' home, she was certain of it, and finding Rob kissing her had been just the excuse he had been seeking.

She searched her mind in an effort to discover just exactly when it had all turned sour. For a while there had been times when, even though they had often been at odds, she had had a kind of instinct that somehow they would make it together in the long run—times when Brand had held her in his arms in the darkness of the night and had made love to her, bringing to blazing life the sweet and wild passions they had known in the past. At such times, she had even been able to forget about Lorraine.

She could not forget her now, however. Once again she was removed from Brand's life while Lorraine was still there, waiting, and surely this second time the other woman would not fail. It was unthinkable that she should, because this time it had been Brand himself who had ordered his wife to leave. He had abruptly lost his vindictive desires to hold her to an empty and meaningless marriage and it could only mean one thing. He had tired of the game; now he wanted a lasting relationship with the woman he truly loved. What other reason could be behind his moving out of their room even before this latest fiasco?

Melody frowned and shifted her position on the lounge chair. Gram and Gramps had both already convinced her that she could not yet file for a divorce. Not until after the baby was born next spring. The child had a right to a legal name. Also, Brand would have to be told.

She had argued with them about that, but Gramps especially had been adamant. She could not expect to support the child as well on any salary she earned when

172

she was able once more to work, as Brand, with all his resources, could. It was both his duty and his right to support his own child, and at last, worn down by male logic, Melody had conceded. But she had still insisted that Brand was not to be informed until the baby was actually born. Until then she wanted nothing from him beyond the money she had removed from her checking account. That, together with her own personal savings, would be enough to see her through until then. She wanted no interference from him at all, either financially or personally.

She glanced upward and watched a sea gull gliding across the boat channel. Why couldn't life be as simple and uncomplicated for humans as it appeared to be for creatures of nature? It seemed that the more one lived, the more difficult life became. She had thought once, when she first left Brand after learning of his affair with Lorraine, that nothing could ever be worse. When Brand walked into that dinner club in Las Vegas and later forced her into marrying him again, she knew it could; and now . . . now she was carrying his child in her womb and her love for him in her heart and the excruciating pain she was experiencing made all that had gone before pale into insignificance.

That evening, while she sat near Gramps, trying to lose herself in a television comedy, Brand telephoned. As Gram spoke to him, Melody tensed, listening to the one-sided conversation. "You're separated again?" Gram asked, sounding convincingly surprised. "Where has she gone? You don't know? But Brand, that's quite irresponsible of you. What if she should happen to need any help?"

Melody winced. Though she could not hear his voice, she could easily imagine what Brand had to answer to *that!* It was almost as though she could feel hostile vibrations emanating across the telephone wires.

She had not been mistaken in her thoughts. Angry sparks glittered in Gram's eyes a few minutes later as she hung up the receiver. "That," she informed the other two needlessly, "was Brand, calling to tell us that you've separated again."

"What all did the boy say?" Gramps asked.

"Not a whole lot," Gram answered. "When he admitted he didn't know for sure where Melody had gone and I pointed out that she might need help, he said he was quite sure that if she did there was a man in Dallas who could take care of her. In fact, he more or less insinuated that was where she was now . . . with him."

"I'm surprised," Melody said huskily from a suddenly parched throat, "that he actually told you about Rob. I didn't think he'd want you to know."

"I'm sure he didn't," Gram snapped, "but when I called him irresponsible it made him angry and he probably said more than he intended. Melody, dear, I don't want to be telling you what to do, but wouldn't it make things better all around if you allowed me to tell Brand you're here with us? And about the baby?"

"No!" Melody's jaw thrust out stubbornly. "No, I don't want him to know yet!"

Gram sighed, threw up her hands in dismay, and looked heavenward. "God help us all! Really, Melody, I'd like to spank you and Brand both!"

Gram didn't, of course, carry out her wish. Even so, during the days and weeks that followed, sometimes she seemed to treat Melody like a little girl, and to her own surprise and amusement she found she rather enjoyed being coddled. Gram sternly ordered her each day to eat what she considered to be the proper amounts of nutritious food for an expectant mother; she saw that she took her vitamins, that she got enough exercise, yet enough rest as well. It had been long years, since before her own mother's death, that Melody had had someone who watched over her every move so solicitously, and somehow it seemed pleasanter and took far less effort just to go along with it.

When October came, she told herself that she ought to make some move toward a future . . . get a place of her own, either in Rockport, in order to be near Gram and Gramps, or someplace entirely different. But the days just slipped past, one after another, and she did nothing at all beyond lending Gram a helping hand around the house. But even that did not add up to much, for Gram had daily help except on the weekends.

She had been there six weeks when Brand telephoned again to say he and Tammy would be coming to visit one Sunday. During the weeks in-between, the elder Traverses had visited them in Corpus Christi a couple of times, sparing Melody the ordeal of bracing for their arrival. But now that they were coming here, Gram did her best to talk Melody into seeing them, but it was to no avail. She might have chanced it if it had been Tammy alone, but Melody quailed at the very thought of seeing Brand again, not to mention braving his rage over discovering she had actually been living with his own grandparents.

The day they were to come, Melody packed a picnic lunch and drove north across the Copano Bay Causeway to Goose Island. It was a beautiful place, a thick woodland of bent and gnarled live oaks. It was a crisply clear and cool day as she wound through the curving roads until she came to the state park. Today she had the park almost to herself, though in the summer it was always packed with picnickers and campers.

She parked near the beach front and walked along the shell-lined shore, breathing in the salty air. There was a young family at one of the tables near the water and she could not help stealing glances at them from time to time. The parents were busily preparing a meal on a camping stove and they suddenly laughed, sharing a secret joke between them; their small son, who appeared about three years old, was racing with his puppy near the water's edge and his shouts of glee pierced the serenity of the day.

Abruptly, Melody wheeled around to the opposite direction and began walking briskly, her hands thrust into her jeans pockets. A lump was lodged in her throat and her eyes were stinging. She had to face facts squarely. Her marriage to Brand was over. There would never come a day for them like there was for that happy couple back there. If Brand ever saw their child at play, it would be when he had "visitation rights" decreed by a court of law.

The sooner she got away from Gram and Gramps, she decided as she walked, the better it would be for all of them. She had them smack in the middle right now and that was unfair. She could not go on depending upon them forever, nor could she indefinitely find a convenient place to hide each time Brand decided to pay them a visit. What if he dropped in unexpectedly sometime?

Any move should be made soon, her thoughts trooped on. Already her middle had thickened to the point where it was difficult to fit into many of her clothes. If she was going to strike out on her own, it had to be now, while she was still mobile and relatively unencumbered.

She thought longingly of her father in Spain. The last letter she had received from him before she left Brand, he and his wife both had pressed her to visit them. She was not sure they would care to have her for a long, extended visit, but, then again, they just might.

She made up her mind that the next day she would check with travel agents about flights. Then, before she did anything definite about booking one, she would telephone them, explain the situation, and go from there.

Slightly cheered that she had at least a definite plan of action in mind, she retraced her route back to the car to fetch her lunch. Even so, it was a long, lonely afternoon before she dared at last to return to the Traverses' home.

Chapter Fourteen

Something was shaking the bed, shaking *her,* and Melody mumbled in protest as she tried to recapture the dream she had been having. It was so beautiful . . . she had been walking on the beach with a child, her child . . . and Brand had been there, too, smiling tenderly upon them both. She turned her head against the soft pillow, wanting the dream to go on forever. Instead, the incessant shaking kept on.

"Please wake up, Melody!" Gram's voice pleaded. It was the note of near hysteria in the voice that finally penetrated through Melody's sleep-fogged brain, bringing her fully awake at last.

Her eyes opened, and when she saw Gram's face, instant concern made her sit bolt upright in the bed. "What's wrong?" she gasped, suddenly alert. "Is Gramps ill?"

"No." Gram, strong, managing Gram, burst into tears.

A cold chill crept up Melody's spine as she threw back the covers and got out of bed. She captured Gram's fluttering hands in hers and ordered sternly, "You must tell me what has happened."

Fortunately, Gramps came into the room just then. "Brand just called," he said grimly. "Tammy was injured in a traffic accident last night. She was riding with some friends." His voice cracked and he swallowed with difficulty before going on. "The others escaped with only minor cuts and bruises, but Tammy was . . . hurt pretty bad. They operated on her late last night and right now Brand says she's holding her own." Now he gazed appealingly into her eyes, both of them totally oblivious to the fact that she was standing there dressed only in a nightgown as she clutched Gram's icy hands. "She's conscious now and then, but she's not out of the woods yet." He stopped, then got on to the heart of the matter. "She's asking for you, Melody. Brand has Dale calling Dallas to try to locate you."

Melody's mouth was dry and cottony. "You didn't tell him I was here?" she asked.

"No. I promised you, but, Melody . . ."

Contrition washed over her. Even in such a tragic circumstance as this, Gramps had not given her away. She could scarcely believe such loyalty. But now it was time to repay her debt to him and Gram, but most of all to

177

Tammy. She forced a smile to her stiff lips, a smile she hoped would somehow instill both Gramps and Gram with some measure of confidence and courage. "Go pour Gram a cup of coffee while I dress," she told Gramps briskly. "We must leave at once."

Gramps's worried face cleared just a little. "Thanks, Melody," he said huskily. "I knew you wouldn't let Tammy down."

Twenty minutes later they were on their way. Melody drove and was glad it gave her something to concentrate on besides the terrible, agonizing fear over Tammy. Gramps, sternly controlling his emotions, had his hands full trying to calm Gram, who simply had fallen to pieces right before their very eyes.

By the time they reached the harbor bridge, Gram was much calmer. She had, she informed them both, just finished a long talk with God and now she was certain that Tammy was going to be all right.

When they walked into Tammy's hospital room a short time later, though, Melody felt her own urgent need to speak to God. Tammy was such a tiny, pale ghost on the bed. Her face was all but concealed by a huge white bandage across her forehead and a rack stood beside the bed, pumping blood into a vein in her arm. Her eyes were closed and she was so still that alarm pulsated through Melody.

For a long moment, she gazed at Tammy as utter despair at her own helplessness swamped over her. She loved this girl so much and there was nothing she could do for her. Tears clogged her throat and she lifted her head. Her tortured eyes met Brand's. He was standing on the opposite side of the bed, staring at her as though he could not believe his eyes. Until that instant, she had scarcely even been aware of his presence. All her attention had been on Tammy.

"How is she?" Gramps asked in a low voice from somewhere behind her.

Brand's gaze held Melody's for a second longer before

178

he shook his head and turned toward the old man. "I don't know." He mouthed the words in pantomime before glancing back toward the bed. Now he spoke aloud in a soft voice. "She comes and goes." He leaned forward and touched Tammy's cheek with a gentle finger. "Tam. Tam, can you hear me, dear?" he asked. "Gram and Gramps are here to see you, and so is Melody."

The grave expression on his face made Melody aware for the first time of just how dreadfully ill he looked. His face was sallow beneath the summer tan that still lingered and he seemed to have aged ten years overnight.

But there was no time to spare thinking about him. She bent forward herself and spoke to Tammy as Brand had done. "Tammy? It's me, honey, Melody."

This time Tammy's eyelashes fluttered upward and she looked directly at Melody. "Hi," she said in a weak thread of a voice.

Melody almost laughed out loud with sheer relief that Tammy could still speak to her. For a minute there she had been so afraid. She smiled and touched Tammy's free hand. "Hi, yourself. Look, Tam, Gram and Gramps are here, too."

Tammy acknowledged her grandparents' presence with a tiny, wan smile just as a nurse came bustling into the room.

"I'm sorry," she said firmly, "but I'm afraid we can't have this many visitors at a time. Only two at once, please."

"Then we'll let you and Gramps stay for a while, Gram," Brand said decisively. "Melody and I will leave."

Tammy's fingers moved beneath Melody's. "You'll come back?" she asked anxiously. "I want you to stay." Her mouth took on a petulant droop like that of a small child.

Melody squeezed her hand and smiled. "Of course I'll stay, honey. After Gram and Gramps visit with you a little while, I'll come back and I'll stay."

"You promise?" Tammy insisted.

"I promise." She bent down and kissed Tammy's paper-white cheek, and then she went from the room.

In the hall, her shoulders slumped and she buried her face in her hands. Brand touched her arm and said quietly, "Come on, I'll buy you a cup of coffee."

"Brand . . ." Her voice was muffled as she allowed him to guide her down the hall. "She's not . . . Tammy isn't going to die!"

"No!" he answered gruffly. "We won't even think it!" he exclaimed. But then he shook his head in a gesture of total despair. "I don't know. The doctors are being very cautious about what they say. She suffered a lot of internal injuries. The operation last night seemed to go on forever."

They got their coffee and found a quiet spot to sit where they could talk undisturbed. "Have you been here all alone since last night?" Melody asked in sharp concern as he rubbed a hand across his tired-looking eyes.

"No. Mrs. Mason was with me until early this morning when I sent her home. She's the lady I hired to live in as Tammy's chaperone or whatever you want to call it. Dale and Marie were here, too," he said unexpectedly, "and they stayed until she came out of the recovery room. Lorraine was here as well for a while."

A tight vise squeezed Melody's heart. She was filled with regret that Lorraine should have had the right to be here with Brand in time of trouble rather than herself. She gave her head a tiny shake and took a sip of the scalding coffee. There was no use in thinking about should-have-beens.

"Where were you?" Brand asked suddenly. "Dale called Wallis last night. We thought you'd be with him, but he told Dale he hadn't seen nor heard from you at all." A puzzled frown lowered his dark eyebrows. "How did Gram and Gramps know where to reach you?"

Melody shrugged in a careless manner. "Oh, I've just kept in touch with them, that's all," she answered vaguely. Now was not the moment to go into the truth about where she had been living. She got to her feet. "Don't you think it's time we went back?" she suggested.

Brand nodded and stood, too, and in silence they headed toward the elevator.

An hour later Brand convinced his grandparents to return home. There was nothing they could do for Tammy themselves, and there was no sense in their staying. Gram, satisfied that Melody would stay at Tammy's bedside herself, finally allowed herself to be coaxed into leaving.

It was a long day. Tammy continued to alternate between short periods of consciousness and lengthy periods of what Melody hoped was restful and healing sleep. She herself sat in an armchair near the bed so that whenever Tammy opened her eyes she could see her at once. Brand occupied the only other chair in the room on the opposite side of the bed.

Sometime during the afternoon Mrs. Mason arrived, bearing flowers, and the three of them stepped outside the door to talk. Melody liked the woman at once, perhaps because she genuinely seemed to care about Tammy and offered to sit with her. It was an offer that was politely refused, however, because neither Melody nor Brand had any intentions of relinquishing their places beside the girl's bed.

But by late that afternoon, Melody insisted that Brand leave for a while. He was bleary-eyed and a day's growth of whiskers stubbled his face. Several times he dozed off in his chair, and finally she went to stand beside him, shaking him gently awake. "You can't go on like this indefinitely," she said softly. "Please, Brand, go home and get some rest. I'll be here."

He started to refuse, but then with a short nod he gave in. "All right, just for a few hours. But you'll call me at once if there's any change?"

"Of course," she assured him.

He stood up, gazed down at Tammy, and then stopped in front of Melody before going to the door. "I . . ." His voice was husky and slightly unsteady. "I haven't told you before, but . . . I'm grateful you came, Melody. I'd like to apologize about . . ."

Melody shook her head quickly. "It's all right, Brand, honestly. Now, just go and get some rest. We can talk some other time."

He gave her a wan smile and nodded again. "All right, then."

Several times during the next few hours, Tammy awoke. The first couple of times she was lucid, asked for water or complained of a headache, but as time went on, when she was conscious she began talking out of her head and thrashing her body in convulsive, uncontrollable movements. Melody had to ring for a nurse and Tammy was administered a sedative, but even that seemed to help little.

Melody was just on the point of picking up the telephone and dialing the house when Brand returned at midnight. He had obviously bathed and changed into fresh clothes, but lines of exhaustion still carved a network around his eyes.

"I was just about to call you," she whispered as she hung up the receiver. "Oh, Brand, I'm so glad to see you!"

"She's worse?" he asked grimly. Just then Tammy began to moan and move uncomfortably in the bed. Her right hand sought to remove the needle that was plastered into the vein of her left arm. Brand moved swiftly to grab Tammy's hand while Melody picked up a damp cloth and began sponging her feverish face.

After that, Tammy sank into a long, lifeless unconsciousness that was more frightening than the wild movements had been. A nurse checked her pulse and hurried away, only to return with a doctor, who promptly thrust Brand and Melody from the room.

They were both pacing the hall when the doctor finally

joined them. "If she pulls through the rest of the night, I believe she'll have it whipped, but . . ."

The "but" hung in the air, and there was no need for him to complete the sentence. In fact, if he did, Melody never heard it. She was running back toward the room, with a prayer in her heart. "She will make it. Dear God, she *must* make it. She will make it."

She had no idea she had spoken aloud until Brand's hand squeezed her shoulder as she stood at Tammy's bedside and he whispered, "You're right. She will make it. Tammy's a fighter."

During the remainder of the long, silent hours of predawn, they both remained at the bedside, and though they did not speak much, there was an accord between them, one single will that was focused on the girl who lay there.

Pink and gold was just beginning to paint the sky outside the window, when Tammy stirred once more. Brand was instantly on his feet bending over the bed and Melody followed suit. A moment later, Tammy opened her eyes, looked from one to the other in a critical manner and said bluntly, "You both look horrible! I can't stand to look at you!"

Melody was laughing and crying at the same time and Brand's face looked as though sunlight had only now broken through a long winter freeze. "You're right, Brand," Melody said as she smiled happily at Tammy. "She's a fighter."

A nurse was sent for and she, too, seemed quite cheered about Tammy's improvement. She went away again to fetch a glass of orange juice Tammy requested and Brand took his turn and insisted Melody go "home" and get some rest. Tammy seconded it with another rude comment about her dreadful looks, so finally Melody agreed, promising to return in the early afternoon.

She took a taxi to the house just as dawn, in all its glory, burst over the bay. She paid off the driver, but instead of going straight inside, she walked around to the back, went down the steps on the bluff, and out onto the pier.

The early morning air was chilling, but she was unaware of any discomfort. She was enthralled at the beauty of this fresh new day. The sun, just rising above the horizon, cast its full light across the calm, glassy waters. The golden tide came frothing gently toward the shoreline.

Her heart swelled with gratitude over such exquisite loveliness, over Tammy's improvement, over the life that was even now growing inside her body. God had given her much for which to be grateful. She must not lose sight of that . . . no matter what!

She turned and made her way back to the house and, using the key she still had, let herself inside. As she climbed the stairs she was too tired to even think about the fact that she had never expected to be here again. She fell asleep almost at once and slept deeply and dreamlessly until noon. After she awoke, she took a quick shower and dressed in a print skirt and blouse she had left behind when she had packed so hurriedly that other day.

Downstairs she found Juanita in the kitchen. The old woman was not surprised to see her because, she explained, Brand had telephoned earlier to say she was there and would be needing a hot meal when she awoke. Melody sat at the kitchen table to eat while Juanita went on to say that Brand had sent very encouraging news about Tammy's condition.

When she had finished eating, Melody said, "That was delicious, Juanita. Now I'd better call a cab and get back to the hospital so Brand can come home for some rest. I'll see you later."

Juanita shook her head. "You sit down again and have another cup of coffee. I'll get Opal to call for you."

"Thanks." Melody obeyed readily. As Juanita left the room, she could hear the doorbell ringing. Shrugging to herself that it was no business of hers anymore, she picked up her cup.

Juanita returned. "Miss White is in the living room and she wants to see you."

Melody hid her consternation and, nodding calmly, went toward the door. Of all times, she thought irritably, to have to see Lorraine again. What rotten luck that she had not left five minutes ago.

Lorraine was pacing the floor in the living room. When Melody entered, Lorraine threw her such a hate-filled look that Melody stopped short.

"I heard you were back," Lorraine rasped. "Just like a bad penny, you keep turning up, don't you? Why don't you clear out for good? Brand doesn't need you . . . or want you! Don't you realize that yet?"

"Maybe you're right," Melody conceded slowly, "but Tammy does need me."

"That kid has to grow up sometime and learn to face disappointments," Lorraine said coldly. Her gray eyes were dark and glittering. "She would soon forget you if you'd just stay out of the way." She took a menacing step closer to Melody. "I think you'd better know something. Brand has asked me to marry him just as soon as you are divorced and I've accepted, so I want you to get out . . . now . . . and never come back! If you don't, I'll . . ."

"You'll what?" A harsh voice asked from the doorway.

Neither of the women had been aware of anything except each other, but now they both turned in shock to see Brand standing there. Melody went white at the grim, forbidding expression on his face. But he was not looking at her at all. He was looking at Lorraine and as Melody glanced back at the other woman herself, she saw that she, too, was pale and shaken. Obviously, Lorraine had not been expecting to see Brand any more than Melody had.

"Brand . . ." Lorraine began tentatively. "I . . ."

He held up a hand and it silenced her. "I want you to clear out your desk at the office today," he said in a soft, dreadfully soft, voice. "I'll call bookkeeping and have them write you a check in lieu of next month's salary."

"But, Brand, you *can't* fire me!" Lorraine protested. "You need me! I was only . . ."

"I would like for you to leave now." Brand broke in on her attempted explanation, still using that dangerously soft voice. "Good-bye, Lorraine."

Lorraine stood rigidly for another moment, but under Brand's implacable gaze she finally gave up. With one more glance of unmasked hatred toward Melody, she went from the room.

The two of them remained standing in tense silence until they heard the slam of the front door. Melody chewed nervously at her lower lip and when Brand's eyes fixed on her at last, she asked, "Why are you here? Who's staying with Tammy?"

He crossed the room until he came to stand just in front of her. "Mrs. Mason's there and Tammy is so much better they both insisted I come home for a while to rest and to tell you not to rush back either." His lips stretched into a weary smile. "Tammy is so much improved that she's already gloating about being able to skip school for a while."

"That's wonderful!" Melody said with an answering smile.

Brand's face went serious again. "You didn't believe Lorraine, did you?" he asked. "About my asking her to marry me?"

Melody could not meet his eyes. She swallowed and stared at the pocket on his shirt. "Why not?" she asked in a flippant manner. "I've known for years that the two of you were having an affair. That was why I ran away from you in the first place."

"What?" Brand's voice was so explosive that in spite of herself she looked at him. His expression was thunderous, his eyes black as an impending storm, and his hands went out to grip her arms so tightly that it hurt. "What in hell are you talking about?" he demanded violently.

Rage surged through Melody and she squirmed, trying to release herself from his grip. "Drop the innocent act,

Brand," she snapped. "I'm sick of it!" In a rushing torrent of bitter words she told him about the night she had tried to telephone him in his hotel room, when Lorraine had answered it. "It was after midnight," she reminded him scornfully, "and when you came on the line, you sounded so sleepy, as though you had just woken up."

"I remember now," Brand said with a frown. "We'd all been to a business dinner meeting . . . Dale, Lorraine, and I . . . and it lasted until almost midnight. When we got back to the hotel, Dale suggested a nightcap, and as I had a bottle of bourbon in my room, that's where we ended up. I was sleepy, but I hadn't been asleep! When the phone rang, Lorraine happened to be sitting beside the table where it was and she just reached out and picked it up before I could get it. When nobody answered, I thought it must have been somebody who had accidentally rung the wrong room. I assure you, Melody," he ended coldly, "that I did not sleep with Lorraine. Not then, not ever! In fact, if I remember correctly, Lorraine left before Dale did that night. If you want to call and have him confirm it, I'll be happy to oblige you." He released her arms and ran a hand through his hair in an irritable gesture "I never gave that trip another thought until this minute because when I got back home you had left me, and nobody knew where you had gone or why. I thought you had left me for another man!"

"Is . . . is that true?" she whispered incredulously. "Oh, dear God, I . . ." Her voice broke. She was appalled at the enormity of what Brand was saying, of what she had done to them both by her wild, jealous, headlong flight.

"Is it true?" Brand said scathingly. "Damn it, Melody, you're the only woman I've ever loved."

"But . . . Lorraine told me herself in a dozen different ways that the two of you . . . that . . ." Her voice trailed off uncertainly.

Brand gave an exasperated sigh. "Oh, I know Lorraine was a bit interested in me, but I swear to you there's never

187

been anything between us. If she told you that, she lied."
His piercing eyes bore into hers so that she could not have
looked away had she tried. "No wonder, then, that you
thought . . ." He broke off and swore softly. "Lorraine is
an excellent secretary and I considered her a good friend
as well until today, but that's all." His lips formed a grim
smile. "I'm not about to tell you I've been celibate during
those years we were divorced, but I was never unfaithful
to you while we were married, not the first time nor this
last time. That's why I couldn't understand your constant
accusations. I was sure you only said it as a defense against
what you had done to me!"

Melody shook her head slightly as she gazed at him with
wonder in her eyes. "Brand, why did you force me to
marry you again?"

Brand shrugged. "I was furious about Dale stealing
company funds so I followed him to Vegas to confront
him, and when I found you there with him, I . . . well, I
realized I had never stopped loving you at all. It was a
spur-of-the-moment decision, my insisting you marry me
again." He gave a rueful grin now. "I intended to scare
the hell out of Dale and to make him pay back what he
had taken, but I never intended seeing him in prison. It
just suddenly seemed like a good way to make you come
back to me."

"Your . . . your bluff worked p-perfectly," Melody said
unsteadily. "I hated you that night."

"Yes." The grin faded; his face took on a haggard look,
emphasizing dark eyes sunken in deathly pallor. "And
many times since. You've told me often enough. You were
right about my desire for revenge. I hoped by marrying
you again that somehow I could make you love me again
as you once had, but my primary reason was based on
pure jealousy. You were engaged to that other man and I
couldn't bear it. If I couldn't have your love I would see to
it that no other man could enjoy it either. That day . . .
that last day, when I found Wallis here in this room,
kissing you, I knew for certain I had lost. You'd been

telling me so often, God knows. Anyhow"—his voice was ragged as he went on—"I knew then that there was no point in my holding you anymore against your will, not even because you had agreed to stay the next three years for Tammy's sake. I know there's a lot to be forgiven, Melody, but I want you to know I'm sorry and that I . . . I truly hope you'll be happy."

She was staring down at her clasped hands, wild hope and elation rushing in to replace the anger that had been there a minute ago. "Thank you," she said softly. "But there's only one thing that can make me truly happy." Slowly, she lifted her head and her eyes were shining. "You. Oh, Brand, I love you so much!"

"Melody! Darling, do you mean it?" Brand's voice cracked over a husky note even as his arms went around her. "But . . . what about Wallis?"

She gave a shaky little laugh. "My engagement to him was a mistake. I knew it the instant you walked into that dinner club that night."

"Then why all the pretense?" he demanded. "Couldn't you *feel* how much I loved you?"

She shook her head. "I suppose we were both too good at the game of acting." She sighed sadly. Her arms slid up across his broad shoulders, her fingers sensuously delighting in the touch of his face before they moved upward to thread through his hair as his head came down and his lips claimed hers with such stark hunger that it left them both quivering and shaken.

At last Brand lifted his head so that their faces were only a fraction of an inch apart. "I ought to beat you," he mumbled lovingly as he pressed her body even closer to his, "for putting me through five years of torture."

She smiled at him in a bemused fashion. "You wouldn't beat an expectant mother, would you now?"

She felt the jolt of shock that went through him. His body went rigid, and if she hadn't been so much in love, she might have termed the expression on his face as ludicrous.

"Darling! You mean . . . you're carrying my . . ." Words failed him and he simply stared numbly at her.

Melody nodded and ran a caressing fingertip lightly across his lips. "I mean I'm going to have your child, Brand," she whispered. "Are you pleased?"

"Pleased?" he asked in a dazed voice. "Pleased?" Now he gave a glad shout. *"Pleased!"* His arms lifted her from the floor and he whirled her around. When he set her down again, there was such a tender light in his eyes that it penetrated to her very soul. "I thought," he said, suddenly grave again, "that you were the most precious thing in the world to me and now . . . now . . ." He crushed her against his chest and his unsteady hand went out to brush her hair away from her face, "now I know what heaven is!"

She felt his body shudder against hers. "What is it?" she whispered. She had never known Brand could be this emotional.

"I came so close to losing you," he said brokenly. "You're going to have my baby and I sent you away from me!"

Melody chuckled, all her own grief of the past few weeks totally dissolved as though it had never been. "I've been living with Gram and Gramps," she confided.

Brand stood back from her and stared at her in disbelief. "You can't be serious! They would have told me!"

"Nope!" She shook her head.

"Did they know about the baby?" His mouth pressed into a hard line.

Once again Melody's finger traced across it, gradually softening it. "Yes, they knew, but there's no use in your being angry with them for not telling you. I had sworn them to secrecy. I must say," she added musingly, "I'm going to miss Gram's coddling. She's been an absolute tyrant about my eating enough and getting plenty of rest."

Brand grinned. "Sounds like Gram, all right. But don't worry. I'll take on the coddling job myself. However,

190

that's not to say Gram and Gramps won't get the scolding they deserve."

"Well, personally, I think you deserve a scold," she told him.

"Why?"

"It's been at least five minutes since you last kissed me and I . . ."

She never got to finish what she was saying because she found herself suddenly being soundly kissed. Her heart thudded against his strong chest and she gave herself up to the thrill of desire and passion that was spreading through her veins.

It was long minutes before they drew apart this time and the light of love in Brand's eyes made her heart race erratically.

"We ought to go over to the hospital and tell Tammy she's going to be an aunt," he said huskily, "and that we're expecting her to do a lot of babysitting in the future, so she'll need to get well soon. And then, Mrs. Travers . . ."

"Yes?"

"Then we're coming home and moving my clothes back into our room where they belong. And then . . ."

"And then?" Her voice drooped. "All that will take so much time."

Brand laughed exultantly. "Come on, you shameless little hussy," he said as he scooped her up into his arms. "We're going upstairs right now."

Melody nestled her head against his neck and contentedly allowed herself to be carried up the stairs.

And neither of them even saw old Juanita standing near the kitchen door, smiling and nodding with approval.

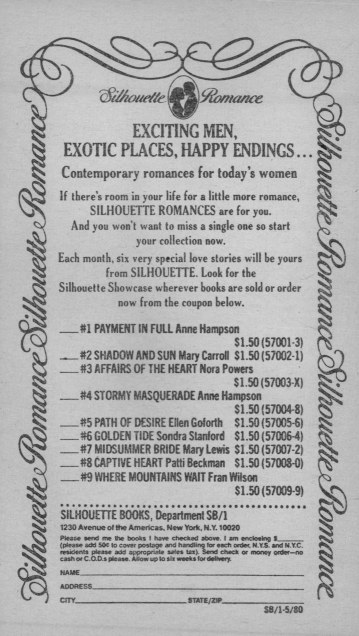